Laszlo Hadron and the Wargod's Tomb
S. L. Dyscadian

Chapter 1

The star IS-G-1522 is, as stars go, a fairly unremarkable one. A red giant somewhere on the edge of the Galaxy's Perseus Arm, it may once have been host to a system of planets but was now home only to a wide belt of barren asteroids. The only thing worth noting about the otherwise desolate star was the presence of a space station nestled within the rocks, a metal ring encircling one of the asteroids, encrusted with various gantries and docking arms - it was a Solar Navy stardock, where the warships of the Solar Commonwealth occasionally stopped off for resupply and refit during their parsecs-long patrols. Several such vessels were docked there today. Among them, its long dagger-like form docked to one of the mooring arms, was a destroyer stretching nearly half a kilometre stem to stern, not including the huge main guns protruding from its prow. The floodlights of the dock illuminated the vessel and picked out the shape of the metres-tall letters engraved in its hull: "SNV DURENDAL". Various little shapes bustled around the ship - robot drones busy pulling up sections of the hull and picking apart her systems, repairing and upgrading. From time to time one of them would hover off to the mooring arm to collect supplies for its task, as one was doing just now. It drifted on a programmed path that took it close to the arm's surface... or rather it would have done had it not hit something and bounced off. Spinning away for a brief moment, it regained its bearings and carried on. Its limited sensors and simplistic programming didn't see anything wrong with the fairly gentle impact, even though a more advanced brain might have been rather worried by the fact that it didn't see anything at all...

Of course, there was something there: another starship clung to the arm's surface. it was much smaller than the Durendal, but in its way no less formidable than the destroyer. It sat safely in the field of its cloaking device, secure in every form of electronic and physical concealment science could conjure, and watched and waited. In the ship's cockpit its pilot sat shrouded in shadow, the rooms of the ship darkened to avoid disrupting the photonic distortion fields. Faintly illuminated by the gentle light of the consoles before her, the woman was slender and athletic. Thick muscle shifted under her black-striped orange fur whenever she moved. A long tail swished idly behind her, her pointed ears twitched subconsciously to track all the little sounds of the cockpit, and filamentous whiskers crowned her white-furred cheeks. Her slit-pupilled eyes flicked back and forth as her screens displayed torrents of data, figures flashing by too fast for the unpractised viewer. She took it all in as easily as if she were reading a newspaper, and eventually satisfied by what she read, she extended an arm to the intercom by her side. There was the faintest hiss as the connection came to life.

"Hacking protocols are up and running, Las, and the cloak's at full capacity," she announced to the person on the other end of the line. "You're good to go."

"Got it. Wish me luck!" came the reply, and elsewhere in the ship another intercom was switched off. This person was taller than the other, clad in an armoured spacesuit coloured in red and white. Double-checking the seals of his outfit, he pressed a button on the room's wall and waited as the airlock's systems drained out the air. As the hiss of atmosphere being extracted faded away and the room's gravity shut itself off, the man named Las pushed himself forward to the airlock's outer door. As the airlock's lights shut off he pushed it open and stepped out into space.

*　　　*　　　*

Most starship maintenance drones aren't especially smart robots. They don't need to be - their range of tasks is very specific and have no need to trouble themselves with much of anything beyond that range. Between that and the invisible ship's hacking protocols, the robots working on the Durendal didn't notice the humanoid figure trailing after one of them on a grapnel line, cloak billowing weightlessly out behind it. The intruder wasn't impeding their work, and so they ignored him as he deftly manoeuvred himself into an unregarded airlock, carrying on with their work as nothing had happened. Their simple computers had no room in their lexicons for the term "space pirate".

The intruder's lexicon, of course, did include that term, because he was one. Interstellar banditry was the very livelihood of the man named Laszlo Hadron, a name notorious throughout much of the Commonwealth's dark underworld, and parts of its lawful side too. It was notorious especially with Elgar Humboldt, Navy captain and commanding officer of the Durendal. Laszlo was not a man the captain remembered with much fondness, and was dedicated to tracking him down and bringing him to justice. As much as Humboldt wanted Laszlo's head though, Laszlo wanted even more to keep it, and had no intention of letting his rival gain an edge. Thus he was taking a rare opportunity to interfere in the Durendal's systems while it was docked and ensure that the ship would be blinded to his own. He stalked cautiously through the ship's corridors and hallways, all but empty while its crew was on shore leave. His long scarlet cloak was drawn about its shoulders, its tech-enhanced weave deadening the soft sounds of his armoured spacesuit and letting him pass stealthily by the few technicians and engineers who were about. Ducking into a doorway, he called up a map of the ship and calculated his route, before clambering into an empty elevator shaft and disappearing into the inner workings of the ship.

*   *   *

The Durendal's computer systems were threaded throughout every part of the ship, but its primary core was a nexus just under the command decks. Responsible for coordinating oversight and control of everything from basic life support to the antiproton reactors and the faster-than-light stardrive, it was a two-storey-tall superprocessor of impressive computing capabilities, regularly seen to by a crew of highly-trained technical officers. Today, however, only a single technician from the stardock was here, overseeing the computer's maintenance cycle. It was mostly a secondary duty, as the station's AI node handled the complex job automatically. The technician was mostly there as an extra pair of eyes, watching idly as monitor programs combed through the ship's code.

They weren't the only one watching, though. As the technician got up and left the room to attend to their own business, a hidden pair of eyes watched them leave. When the door closed behind them, a ceiling panel swung open and Laszlo dropped out of a hollow in the ceiling. He rappelled carefully down the superprocessor's side and touched down on the deck, before rising to his full height and sweeping his cloak back behind his shoulders. Sparing a brief glance towards one of the room's security cameras, its sight subverted by his own ship's hacking protocols, he made his way over to the technician's console. Peering at the screen, he grinned to himself - the poor sap hadn't even logged out! He settled into the console's chair and took the liberty of retracting his helmet. As it folded swiftly into the collar of his suit, he tapped at the terminal's keys. He spared a hand for his earpiece.

"You there, Isis?" he asked.

"I read you, Las," came the reply. "We ready to link up?"

"In but a moment..." Laszlo worked at the terminal, opening the Durendal's systems up to connection to his own ship. "Alright, the network's open. Work your magic."

Isis was silent, but Laszlo trusted her skill and waited. As seconds passed, he stared idly at his face reflected in the mostly black screen. It was a pretty good face in his opinion, with an angled jawline he liked to think of as heroic, lined by the trimmed sideburns that descended from short-cut reddish-brown hair and to the goatee that he'd lovingly maintained for most of his adult life. His eyebrows arched itself by reflex over bright green eyes, implanted sub-optic lenses glinting when the light caught them just so, until he was brought back to the moment by a trill from the console, as the interface completed itself. With total untraceable access to the Durendal's systems granted to him, Laszlo began his work in earnest. Any starship had a unique and distinct profile to any other ship's sensors, and his own vessel was no exception, even with its numerous stealth devices. But, with just the right data-blocking, he could exclude that profile from being recognised by the Durendal and effectively blind the destroyer to it. He stared intently at both the console and his wrist-panel, uploading programs and altering code, integrating a custom system patch into the computer's maintenance cycle. With a little luck it would be absorbed into the existing code along with all the other little upgrades that an overhaul like this entailed, and thus pass unnoticed.

Finishing his typing, he leaned back in the chair and watched as lines of code flickered on and on. He made one last check of his work, and his eye was caught by something unusual. Recent logs had been turned up in the course of modifying the ship's systems, that seemed to indicate events outside the ship's normal schedule. Laszlo knew he ought not to linger and should just get out of there, but curiosity was one of his worst vices. Weighing things up in his mind, he soon ignored his practical side and opened the log files. Most of it was the usual report from the Durendal's standard patrol operations, until it had been called to assist in a pirate attack on a ship from the Commonwealth Department of Operations, the Amber Eye. This in itself was strange, Laszlo thought, because most pirates wouldn't take the risk of taking on a ship from the Commonwealth's prime intelligence organisation. Intrigued, he read on, and learned that after the Durendal had chased off the pirate attackers, she had taken on the crew of the stricken ship as it was too damaged to carry on. Along with this, the ship's captain had given to Captain Humboldt what they had been delivering, which was--

"What are you doing here?!"

The sound of the technician's voice cut straight through Laszlo's concentration. Working by long-practised instinct, he shot to his feet and snatched a neuro-disruptor from his belt. Before the technician could properly react, a blazing stun bolt hit them in the chest and left them sprawled unconscious on the floor. Laszlo strode over to them, grabbed them under the shoulders and dragged them over to a tool cupboard. He shoved the technician inside the cabinet and shut them inside. Leaning against the door and drumming his fingers, Laszlo pondered his situation.

"Shit."

"I'm guessing we've got problems?"

Isis's tone was resigned, but not reproachful. Nonetheless, Laszlo swallowed guiltily.

"Almost got caught out by a technician. I stunned them and now they're enjoying this tool cabinet."

Isis frowned to herself, but took it in stride. Expecting things to go wrong was the crucial precaution of this kind of job. Her thoughts slid smoothly into damage control mode.

"Okay. You'll probably have a few minutes before anyone misses them. Just stick to the plan and get out of there."

Laszlo stepped away from the cabinet and resealed his helmet. "Yes, yes... I just want to check something out first."

"Las..." Isis chided wearily. She knew where this was going.

"It's only a little thing! It'll be fine."

Isis didn't bother to try dissuading him. "Just try to stay out of more trouble, okay?" she sighed without much hope, as Laszlo shot a grapnel up to the vent in the ceiling he'd entered through and clambered back into the Durendal's innards.

*   *   *

The captain's office of most Navy ships was directly behind the bridge, at the very top of the ship. With all the officers who might otherwise have reason to enter the room on leave, the room was empty and the door locked. This wasn't necessarily an obstacle to the determined visitor however, as the business end of a spindly tool reached out of a ventilation panel in the room's corner. Metallic filaments found their way to the panel's securing bolts and unfastened them, allowing the tool's owner to open the panel and crawl out of the service duct. Laszlo deftly unfurled himself as he rose and checked around the room reflexively. An elliptical room, the office was dominated by a wide and impressive desk in the room's centre. Simple chairs lined one side, facing the rather more imperious-looking chair appropriate to the ship's captain, which was flanked by monitors and consoles. Laszlo stepped around the desk's end and settled himself into the almost throne-like seat.

The desk's surface was mostly bare, save for a few items of stationery, a stray datapad, a few framed photos of Captain Humboldt's loved ones, and a scale model of the Durendal. Laszlo hadn't really expected Elgar to simply leave the item from the Department ship out for everyone to see, and as such he began going through the desk's drawers. It was mostly mundane things - more datapads, assorted paperwork, a spare service pistol - until finally he came across what he was looking for. He smiled broadly and snatched it from the drawer.

It was a datacell - the Solar Commonwealth's primary means of physical data storage. A thin sheet of crystal an inch along either side, held in a metal and plastic frame, storing terabytes of data encoded in densely packed microscopic laser-etched patterns. This particular datacell was a fairly standard 500-terabyte model. It wasn't really much to look at, even as colours flashed through the crystal as it turned in the light, but as soon as Laszlo's fingers had touched the object a subconscious tingle ran through them. A lifelong career of piracy had given him something of a sense for things of value, and anything that pirates would risk trying to steal from a Commonwealth spy ship was unquestionably very valuable indeed. Just holding it, Laszlo was already conjuring up ideas of what to do with it, and what to do with the money...

Lost in his scheming, he mentally shook himself and returned to the moment. He had what he'd come for, and now he just needed to get out without--

"Intruder alert! Intruder alert! Unauthorised personnel have boarded the Durendal! All personnel to security stations!"

As klaxons blared and alarm lights flashed around him, Laszlo's shoulders slumped in frustration. So much for Plan A!

"Las, the entire station just went to high alert," Isis chimed in. "You've been discovered, haven't you?"

"Yes," Laszlo sighed in exasperation, already getting back up to leave.

"Of course you did." Isis' tone was unmistakeably that of a verbal eye-roll. "Alright. You need to get off the Durendal now. They'll have all the airlocks locked down... probably the internal doors too... and all the maintenance hatches..."

"I don't suppose we could save the inevitable "I told you so" for when I'm back on the Wyvern, could we?" Laszlo groused, grunting as he worked his ways back into the service hatch.

"Oh fine, if you must ruin my fun..." Isis pretend-pouted. "I really did tell you, though."

"Duly noted. Now shut up and find me an escape route, if you'd be so kind."

"Okay, your best bet's going to be the upper hangar bay, at the back of Deck 3. With repairs going on, they'll probably be something in there you can fly out of there. Provided you can get the bay doors open."

"I'll worry about that part when I get there." Crawling his way through the duct, Laszlo could hear the clatter of security personnel hurrying urgently to and fro, even over the sound of the alarms. Listening out for the opportune moment, Laszlo slid out of an open panel and fell into a crouch on the deck plating. He glanced this way and that, keeping his eyes and ears open for danger.

"I've got routes for you," Isis said. "Sending them to you now."

Laszlo lifted his arm and called up the data on his wrist panel. A map of the Durendal's command decks appeared in hologram before him, with brightly coloured lines marking out possible routes. Laszlo picked one and set off at a jog, hoping he wouldn't run into any more trouble. He rounded a corner and...

"Wh-- HEY!!"

At the sight of five Naval marines standing right before him, Laszlo skidded to a clumsy halt and hastily took off back in the other direction. It was only a few seconds before the surprise wore off and the marines started after him. Stun bolts impacted around the rapidly retreating pirate, drowning out the sound of his frantic swearing.

Today was really not going his way.

*   *   *

Ships of the Greatsword-class like the Durendal possessed three hangar bays - two on either flank for its complement of starfighters, and another at the back of the command decks intended for shuttles, transports, and the like. With the Durendal undergoing repairs, it was in a rare state of disarray - crates of supplies and materials piled around small cargo lifters, deck plating pulled up to access the machinery and systems therein. It was a distinct contrast to its usual military efficiency, and it was perfect for Laszlo to get around stealthily.

Marines covered the massive room in careful search patterns, trying to root the interloper out, and Laszlo crept around the room one step ahead of them - but only just. Even with his quick feet, it was occasionally only the holographic camouflage in his spacesuit that stopped him from giving himself away.

Sneaking around crates and clambering up girders, he was carefully plotting his escape plan. The fact that so many systems were exposed allowed him to do what needed to be done. Leaning out from a specific panel in the wall, he made a quick inventory of all the transports landed in the hangar. He might have preferred to blast out in a stolen starfighter - it was the way he generally liked to do things - but such ships weren't often used in starship repair, so he only had cargo lifters and utility pods to choose from. He picked out what he judged the best option and began to make his way around the marines searching for him.

He dropped quietly down from the panel, and alighted on the deck. Moving by practised instinct, he deftly worked his way across the hangar - ducking behind a crate, swinging down around the lip of the platform, clambering across a girder. He reached the pod he'd chosen and, with tremendous care and caution, manually pried open the entry hatches. He knew that no matter how quiet he could have been in doing so, someone would have heard the pneumatic hiss of those doors, so he wasted no time in getting to work at the controls, doing what he needed to do. With any luck, he had just enough time to...

"Turn away from the controls and exit the pod with your hands up."

There it was. Laszlo turned slowly, hands raised, to see the doors open and a number of marines at the hatch, their weapons trained squarely on him.

"Whatever you say, chief," Laszlo answered with airy calm. "But first, would you be so good as to give me a count of five?"

Laszlo carefully enunciated the word "five", and it set something off in the panel he'd modified a few moments ago. There was a large yet quiet mechanical sound, and the marines looked up to see what was happening.

"What the-- the doors!"

"Someone get them closed again!"

As some of the marines at the hatch hurried off to reseal the main doors, the leader of the group renewed his grip on his pistol.

"This is your last warning!"

Laszlo shrugged. "No? Suit yourself, then. Five!"

Things happened quickly after that - before the marines could even properly register the explosion of a certain wall panel, the hangar was filled with a sudden wind as the containment field failed and the bay was suddenly exposed to the vacuum of space.

Between the confusion of deafening klaxons and the general furor of the marines to get things under control, Laszlo was able to turn back to the utility pod's controls undisturbed. Scrambling into the pilot's seat, he brought his fist down on the starter button. The pod rocketed off the landing platform and hurtled out into space.

Of course, Laszlo pondered to himself as he gazed out of the still-open hatch, this move could only get him so far - literally. No military crew would be careless enough to leave an unattended craft fully fuelled just in case some pirate needed a handy escape route. What little fuel the pod had carried had been consumed in that brief full-power burst, and it left the little vessel drifting swiftly away from the Durendal, unguided and uncontrolled, with a helpless Laszlo along for the ride.

"Say, Isis... ?"

"I'm on it, Las," came the prompt reply. "Hold on tight, there'll be a bit of a bump."

Laszlo turned to face the front of the craft in time to see a large metal claw coming straight at him. The pod juddered as the claw's micro-gravitic field drew it into its grip, wrapping its digits around the little round ship. With its grasp secure, the claw tugged the pod back and began drawing it into its source: a cargo bay whose opening seemed to be an aperture in completely empty space.

It was the Wyvern, of course - the dimmed interior of its cargo bay was the only break in its cloaking field. Laszlo clambered out of the pod and onto the claw itself. Holding onto the bundle of thick cables trailing up to the spool hanging from the cargo bay ceiling, he placed his feet against one of the claw's broad fingers, and as he entered the cargo bay's gravity field, he found himself standing on it.

As the pod cleared the rim of the bay's opening, containment field fizzing gently around its shape (unlike the Durendal's, this field was set to permeable), the doors slid shut and closed with a gentle thud. Standing in the cargo bay waiting for Laszlo, a cat-eared figure sauntered up to the pod. Her arms were crossed, her tail swished from side to side, and her eyebrow was arched in an accusing way.

"So when you said this op was going to go entirely to plan... ?" Isis Lagato asked, with just a hint of reproach.

"Things went perfectly to plan, Isis," Laszlo said with smooth assurance, retracting his helmet and jumping down from the claw to the deck before her. "Just not quite to plan A, is all."

Isis shook her head. "Why in space do I put up with you?"

Laszlo put on his most dashing smile. "Because I'm endearingly pathetic and you know I'd be utterly done for without you?" Isis couldn't help but smirk, and the two left the cargo bay for the cockpit.

"So what did you manage to get done? I've never seen you this chirpy about a failed mission."

Laszlo half-turned as he entered the cockpit, fishing the datacell out of his pocket and handing it to Isis. "I did come across a little something - what do you make of this?"

Isis took the datacell and turned it over in her fingers. She grabbed a nearby computer tablet and slotted it in, only for it to beep indignantly at her. She blinked in surprise.

"Well, whatever it is, the encryption just completely wiped my tablet," she said, removing the datacell and putting the now-useless tablet to one side. "This has to be top-level stuff. Where the hell did this thing come from?"

"Up until the Durendal interceded, it was in the process of being stolen by pirates from a Department of Operations ship. So whatever it is, I'm guessing it's something good."

Isis nodded, frowning to herself. "Possibly... or maybe it's something that'll get us in a lot of trouble with the law."

Laszlo's near-manic grin told her that he probably considered these two options pretty much the same thing. Taking their seats at the Wyvern's controls, Isis began to take the invisible ship to the edge of the system's asteroid field, to a point where a safe lightspeed course could be plotted.

"In any case, I almost got captured getting this thing off the Durendal, so I'd like to do something with it just to see what all the fuss is about," Laszlo said.

"In that case, we'll probably want to find a computer that can decrypt it without being fried."

The two exchanged glances over the central console, both arriving at the same conclusion.

"Mat?"

"Mat."

Isis turned to the navigation console and laid in the course. On the edge of IS-G-1522's asteroid field, a safe distance away from the stardock, the Wyvern's cloaking field shut down, leaving the streamlined vessel visible for a few seconds, before it vanished into lightspeed in a bright blue flash...

Chapter 2

It is an undeniable fact that, beyond a certain radius of a star, space is dark. Even then the sky is filled with the myriad illumination of the stars, their distant pinprick glow keeping onlookers company. But this is only true within the boundaries of galaxies, and they are bright islands in an unfathomable ocean of nothingness. Past the rim of the Milky Way, there are no stars, there is no light. The night is unending and unbroken - truly dark.

Out on the Galaxy's edge, where the last few stars thin out into this endless void, there is very little worth visiting. The sparse scattering of stars, dozens if not hundreds of light-years apart, hardly ever hosted any planets of mineral or environmental significance. For the most part, no-one thought it worth the effort to come out here. Thus, it was a good place to keep certain things secret, away from prying eyes in populated space.

There was a sudden burst of brilliant blue energy, fading quickly into the background darkness - the telltale flash of exotic radiation of a starship appearing in normal space. It was the Wyvern, arriving at its destination from IS-G-1522. Laszlo and Isis were no strangers to the sight of the intergalactic void, because there were a number of pirate outposts along the edge of the Galaxy. But it wasn't one of those that they were paying a visit to. Something else hung in space before them...

"Jump complete. We're getting a signal."

To anyone who hadn't seen them before, the readings from the Wyvern's sensors would have been dismissed as a malfunction. Surely nothing could have been that big?

"Yep, it's Mat. Receiving an approach vector."

It should have been impossible - no sensibly conceivable object should have had that kind of mass without either igniting into a star or being crushed by its own gravity. And yet, no matter what science might try to say, there it was - a dark, cold sphere the size of a star.

"Vector resolved - bringing her in for landing."

The Wyvern's engines flared and it flew on towards the impossible object. No detail on its lightless surface could be discerned by the naked eye - if it could, it might have appeared to be a tremendous wall in space, seemingly infinite in scale - until a glow appeared before the ship. As the Wyvern approached the light grew, first into a circle then into a widening ring, as the sphere's surface opened up into a tunnel. The Wyvern dove in and flew on through the passage in the sphere's miles-thick outer shell. Lines of light guided the ship to another opening delineated by a glowing ring. The Wyvern emerged from the tunnel into the sphere's inner space, and found itself in a bubble of atmosphere at precisely the same temperature and pressure as the ship's interior. It followed around the ship as it cruised ever more slowly over the inner surface, landing gear extending for touchdown. Moving beneath the ship was a pool of light, matching the vessel's speed and path, almost literally shadowing it. Soon enough the Wyvern set itself down on this mobile island of light, and found it to be as firm as any landing platform.

As the Wyvern's engines cooled, the portside airlock opened and Laszlo and Isis stepped out onto their ship's wing. As they did, more light wakened in the ground and surged up to the wing's lip. This light seemed liquid in both form and motion, flowing into place as though one could pour sunlight into a glass, and yet it supported the pair just as well as any solid object as it formed into a flight of stairs under their feet. As she descended, Isis looked upwards and saw what seemed at first glance to be a night sky full of bright stars. The panorama of glimmering points were just a little too ordered to complete the illusion, however - arrangement and twinkling both according to some inscrutable pattern - and the more Isis looked at them, the more she was reminded of the status lights of a computer... or perhaps neural impulses moving through a living brain?

"I like what you've done with the place, Mat," Laszlo said. He was also looking up at the sky, although he couldn't help but get the feeling that it was actually an unfathomably distant ceiling.

"Thank you, Laszlo!" The reply was spoken by a warm and friendly voice that seemed to emanate from everywhere at once. "I'm glad you find my accommodations suitable. But where are my manners? Please, take a seat, makes yourselves comfortable!"

With this invitation, a pair of chairs rose from the ground before the Wyvern. Rather than being more constructs of fluid light, these seemed to be perfectly ordinary armchairs - paisley upholstery slightly worn as if by frequent use, and invitingly comfy-looking. Laszlo and Isis accepted the invitation and sank gratefully into the soft cushions. A small table emerged quietly before them, complete with teapot, cups, and a plate of biscuits.

"It's good to see you again, Mat," Isis said to the seemingly sourceless voice that had spoken, as she added a couple of spoonfuls of sugar to her tea. "How have you been?"

"I keep quite well, Isis, thank you," came the answer, this time coming from the glowing form that was coalescing into being before the two. It was a simple shape, round and nebulous like a sphere of thick mist, wreathed in a brilliant corona tinged at the edges with blue. Yet the light cast by this little star was gentle and comfortable - bright enough to clearly illuminate the area, but soft enough to look into without discomfort.

"It's a quiet life here on the edge of nowhere, alone with my thoughts," Mat continued, their star-like avatar hovering around eye level for their guests. "But shall we get to business? I gather this isn't simply a social call - how can I help you?"

Laszlo set his cup down and dug into one of his belt's pouches. "Well, we were trying to sabotage a Commonwealth warship's sensors - didn't go terribly well, incidentally..." he began, as his searching fingers found the datacell and pulled it out for Mat to see, "and I came across this in the process."

An invisible impulse lifted the cell gently from Laszlo's unresisting fingers and brought it up to Mat. The little object turned over and over, as if in the fingers of someone closely studying it.

"A datacell," Mat observed, speaking half to themselves, "capacity of a few hundred terabytes, Commonwealth Department of Operations markings..." The cell stopped turning and lowered a little. "What's on it?"

"We were kind of hoping you could tell us," Isis said. "I tried to access it myself, but it fried my tablet."

"Did it really? My goodness. That would indicate some very powerful encryption. If you'll allow me a moment..."

A shaft of light shone from Mat's form and through the crystal core of the datacell, casting geometric rainbow patterns on Laszlo and Isis.

"Yes... just as I thought..." Mat said after a moment of analysis. "It's no wonder this datacell destroyed your system, Isis. It's locked down with Omega-grade encryption."

Laszlo paused with a biscuit halfway to his mouth, his interest now thoroughly piqued. "Omega-grade?" he echoed, leaning forward in his seat.

"Indeed so," said Mat. "The Department of Operations' highest-level data protection system. Designed to actively resist and retaliate against any unauthorised access."

"I guess you were right, Las," Isis remarked. "It MUST be something good."

"Undoubtedly," Mat said. "The Department wouldn't use such a system lightly. Of course, it's no match for me," they said, a note of smugness entering their voice. "Still, it might take a while to decrypt everything. I'll see if I can give you a little now..."

Mat lapsed back into silence as they returned to reading the datacell. Laszlo and Isis were silent too, barely even paying attention to their tea as they waited. Eventually the light-shaft dimmed and the datacell lowered, as Mat concluded their analysis. Their air of congenial host seemed to have faded somewhat, and a feeling of seriousness had descended over them.

"It would appear that the Department of Operations is taking a considerable interest in the excavation of Sagittarian ruins on the planet Eurus," they finally announced.

Laszlo's brows furrowed in thought. "Sagittarian... ? Well, if the Commonwealth's interested in it enough to bring in the Department, then it can only mean..."

"... the Extinction."

"What Extinction?" Isis asked. "I'm hearing a capital "E"."

"Well, the Sagittarians ruled an interstellar empire about two million years ago," Laszlo began. "It was great and mighty and all that, as big in its heyday as the Solar Empire... and one day it just vanished. The whole thing was brought down practically overnight."

"What happened to them?" Isis asked.

"It's not fully clear, but the evidence points to a war of some kind," Mat answered, "a tremendous, terrible war fought against, or by, or for, something called the Wargod."

"The Wargod?"

"Some sort of ultimate weapon," Laszlo continued, "created by the Sagittarians to battle an unparalleled existential threat."

"Or perhaps it WAS the threat. Very little Sagittarian records exist, and we don't have a clear enough picture of the situation to do more than guess."

"But the legend says that that thing's still out there somewhere, sealed in the so-called "Wargod's Tomb", waiting to be rediscovered."

Isis shifted in her seat, as she realised the history weighing on the situation. "So why haven't I heard anything about this before?"

"As I said, there aren't enough surviving documents to form a definite history," Mat said, "and some people don't even believe it happened at all. The Wargod and the Sagittarians themselves are as much myth as history."

"But if the Commonwealth is taking an interest in them all of a sudden," Laszlo said thoughtfully, "and keeping it quiet like this... something's got them scared. There must be something to it after all." He picked the datacell up off the table and gazed at it thoughtfully.

"So, what do you reckon?" Isis asked. "Take this info to the black market, sell it off to the highest bidder? Ransom it back to the Commonwealth? Either way, we could make a fortune off it."

"Maybe..." Laszlo murmured in answer, not looking away from the datacell, "but d'you know what I rather want to do?"

"Abandon it in deep space and keep our noses out of a situation clearly way over our heads?"

Laszlo gave Isis an odd look at this suggestion, but laughed when he saw her grinning. "Well, we probably ought to, but since when have I ever turned down a good mystery?"

"Never in all the years I've known you," Isis said, rolling her eyes with a knowing smile. "What planet did you say those ruins were on, Mat?"

"Eurus, in the Outer Province," Mat replied, a similar smile evident in their own voice. "Though if I might make one request, might I accompany you on this little adventure?"

Laszlo was surprised by this. "Well, we'd love to have you come along, Mat, but, er..." - his gaze turned skyward for a moment - "... you're just a smidge too big to fit inside the Wyvern."

Mat chuckled softly. "Don't worry, I'd not expect you to make that much concession for me!" Something spherical appeared on the table with a small yet heavy "plunk". "Just bring this along with you to the ruins on Eurus' surface, and I shall see what there may be to be seen."

*   *   *

Commander Leurak's claws beat a staccato rhythm on the arm of xir chair, as xe waited with nervous impatience. Around xem, most of the rest of the Durendal's senior officers busied themselves preparing the destroyer for launch, occupied with the routine work of running the ship. Without any real need for the first officer to personally intervene, xe had nothing to do but wait.

The Durendal's bridge was a round room beneath a transparent dome. Facing inward around a large circular holoprojector in the room's centre were a series of consoles, with a pair of suitably important-looking chairs for the captain and first officer - the latter specially adapted for Leurak's arthropodal Ylerakk anatomy - facing toward the front of the ship. To Leurak's left was the navigation console, where a young Human officer was analysing course projections. He glanced away from his holographic screens at the sound of Leurak's fitfully tapping fingers.

"Feeling nervous, sir?"

Leurak snapped out of staring into space and stopped drumming on the furniture. "Uhh-- well, yes. Sorry Chris, I wasn't disturbing you, was I?"

Christopher Sandersby shook his head. "Not at all, sir. You just seemed ill at ease, that's all."

Leurak let out a gentle sigh and curled one of xir antennae around xir finger. "It's that security breach we suffered a while ago. I'm not looking forward to answering for it to the Captain..."

"I don't think you need to be so worried, Leurak." The interjecting voice, gravelly and Slavic-accented, belonged to Oleg Volkash, the Durendal's gunnery chief, who had sauntered over from his console opposite the captain's chair to join in. "The Captain will understand - if he does punish you for this, it won't be more than a minor discommendation."

"Besides, you had weapons training, didn't you?" This voice was Vren Torzay, the Vanda communications officer. Ink flowed under her translucent blue skin in decorative patterns as she gestured with long, sinuous fingers. "You would have been halfway across the station in the firing range. What could anyone have expected you to do?"

"I guess so..." Leurak mumbled to xemself. "But he's definitely not going to like this."

Any speculation on this matter was ended at this point, as the doors opened and the Captain himself stepped onto the deck. Elgar Humboldt was a fresh-faced man in his mid-twenties, of roughly average height and slender build, who wouldn't have looked terribly special in most scenarios. But in bearing the mantle of a captain in the Solar Navy, he carried himself with a naturally imperious, almost regal bearing that transcended his physical presence, an instinctive confidence that commanded immediate respect. He had been awarded his rank less than two years ago and was the youngest Human captain in the First Fleet, but he had taken to it as though it had been made specifically for him. If you had told someone that he had been born with his captain's star, they might well have believed you.

As Elgar approached his chair his officers stood to attention and saluted. He snapped off his own salute in turn.

"At ease, crew."

The officers all took their posts, and Elgar himself settled into his own chair. At his side, Leurak made a quiet noise that was the Ylerakk equivalent of clearing the throat.

"Welcome back, Captain. Did you enjoy your shore leave, sir?" xe politely asked.

"I did, Mx. Leurak, thank you for asking," the Captain replied. "And aside from the security breach, was the Durendal alright in my absence?"

"Er, yes sir. Apart from that, everything's in fine shape."

"Good to hear, Commander!" The Captain studied a holoscreen for a moment, before steepling his fingers and regarding his first officer with a serious expression. "Speaking of which, perhaps we should address the matter of the breach?"

It was the moment Leurak had been dreading, but xe took a deep breath and soldiered on. "I'm sure you've read my report already, sir. There's not really much more to tell. Security footage of the incident was wiped by an unknown source, and internal sensors were offline for maintenance, but personnel report that the individual was wearing a white armoured spacesuit with a red cloak..."

A sudden flash of anger passed briefly over Captain Humboldt's face, and he had to take a steadying breath before continuing. "Was anything damaged during the assault?"

"N-no, sir," Leurak answered, startled by his superior officer's suddenly darkened expression, "at least, nothing we weren't able to fix before your return. It seems the intruder was trying to modify the ship's sensor code, but we were able to reinstall from the master default before your return. Oh, and I'm told the technician found in the tool cupboard wasn't seriously injured."

"Well, good. Although they'll need some reminding of proper data security," the Captain said, distracted by his own thoughts. "Anything reported stolen?"

"All standard supplies and equipment are accounted for, sir. We weren't able to track all the intruder's movements though, and some of the compromised security footage came from your office, sir..."

"I'd feared as much..." the Captain said half to himself. His manner was agitated as he rose to his feet again and he barely looked at his first officer as he spoke. "I'll leave you to see to the business of launching the Durendal for now, Mx. Leurak - I have something I need to attend to."

Confused but compliant, Commander Leurak took to xir duties, as Captain Humboldt retreated into his office. The door closed behind him and shut out the sounds of the bridge, as Elgar rounded his desk and settled into his chair. Holoscreens appeared automatically before him at his approach, but he ignored them and instead leaned down for the bottom drawer. He pulled it open and found... nothing. It was gone.

Cursing under his breath, Elgar dug through what was in the drawer, then pulled open the other drawers and rifled impatiently through them too, in the vain hope that he'd simply misplaced the object of his search. But he had no luck, and with a loud sigh he was forced to concede that it was indeed gone. He dropped his peaked cap on the desk and ran his hands through his hair in exasperation, before slumping back into his chair.

"Bugger."

For a moment, Elgar simply sat and stewed in his frustration, but after a moment he pulled himself together. No matter how little he wanted to, he needed to report this. He donned his cap again and turned to one of his holoscreens, calling up the comms. He entered the code for the Department of Operations, and waited as the connection was made.

"This frequency is reserved for priority use," a synthesised voice announced in reedy monotone. "Misuse will incur penalties up to and including suspension from duty and incarceration. Please submit name, rank, and serial number for evaluation and vocal analysis."

"Elgar Humboldt, Captain, serial number FG-495626-B," he recited distinctly.

The system was silent for a moment as it analysed his voice. "Thank you Captain Humboldt, your vocal pattern has been verified and your communique has been accepted. Please stand by to speak to a Department agent."

"Hello, Captain." A natural voice this time, definitely belonging to a person. But still, no face appeared on the screen, just a waveform of the voice. "I take it this is in regards to the Amber Eye?"

"Yes... I'm afraid the item I took delivery of has been stolen."

"I see." If the voice's owner was upset or angry, their level tone didn't betray it. "Do you know who took it, or where it is?"

"I believe it's currently in the hands of Laszlo Hadron, but I can't say where he might have taken it."

"Hadron, eh? Our records indicate that you have a history with this man..."

"I didn't give it to him myself, if that's what you're implying," Elgar said, affronted.

"Not at all, Captain, forgive me," the voice continued. "But you do know him, so you could be a useful judge of his character. Can you offer any insight as to his next move?"

"I used to know him..." Elgar muttered, mollified but sullen. He cleared his throat and rubbed his chin in thought. "But if he hasn't changed much since then... well, worst-case scenario would be that he's managed to crack the cipher and read the data. I should think then that he'd stick his nose in, get himself involved." He scoffed to himself. "He never could resist an adventure."

"You're certain of your conclusion?"

"Quite certain, yes. He may be trying to sell it on instead," Elgar said, doubtfully, "but I can't really see him doing that. His partner, maybe... no. No, I should think they'll be trying to get involved in things."

"Very well. We'll operate under that assumption for now. You will proceed to Sel'Akis as previously ordered. Vice Admiral Elrey does not need to be updated on the situation, nor does your ship's log."

Elgar's brows furrowed. "Sel'Akis? But I was going there to deliver the datacell. I don't have it anymore."

"Your presence is required there in accordance with the larger scope of this affair," the voice continued smoothly, "but I'm not at liberty to discuss the reasons any further."

Elgar was unimpressed. "Well, I'll cooperate with the Department, but I'd like it noted that I do so under protest. I don't much care for being left in the dark like this."

"I apologise for being cryptic, but please understand the need for discretion. All will become clear in due course. Department of Operations out."

The connection was closed and the screen went blank. Elgar stared at it for a moment, then let out a sigh. He'd heard the old saw about how the Department of Operations "moved in mysterious ways", but it was something else altogether to be caught up with them, dragged along without knowing where you were going. Wondering if this was how pawns on a chessboard felt, he shook his head and returned to the bridge.

Commander Leurak looked up as the Captain sat back down beside xir. "We're underway, sir, all systems green across the board. Is everything as it should be?"

Captain Humboldt paused for the briefest moment as he considered his answer. "Let's just say that everything is as expected, Commander," he answered carefully, thinking it best not to explain his dealings with the Department - not that he had much to divulge, anyway. "We'll proceed as before. Mr. Sandersby, lay in a course for the Sel'Akis system."

"Aye aye, sir," the young lieutenant-commander replied. "Plotting course now."

"Ms. Larroe, are we prepared for transit?" the Captain continued.

"The stardrive is charged and ready, sir," the Durendal's chief engineer answered, her otter-like Suura head appearing in hologram above the bridge's central projector - her post was down in the primary reactor room, rather than on the bridge. "We can initiate jump at your discretion."

"Very good," Humboldt said with a curt nod, dismissing the hologram. "Mr. Sandersby, engage."

In space, the Durendal turned towards its unimaginably distant destination, and with a brilliant flare from its engines and a blue flash, it leapt away.

*   *   *

Eurus was a smallish planet on the southeastern outskirts of the Solar Commonwealth's Outer Province. It had a nice enough climate range by most species' standards, aside from its dramatic dust storms, as well as decent resources for agriculture and mining, but not enough to merit any major colonisation effort. Even the Tygoethans had ignored it in their war against the purportedly encroaching Solar Empire two hundred years ago. Eurus was a quiet backwater that would have been virtually unheard of by most people in the Galaxy, were it not for the planet's sole claim to fame: it was home to the most extensive and best preserved Sagittarian ruins ever discovered. To find any artifact of this ancient civilisation was remarkable, given how little remained of them, but the Euran ruins spanned over a full square mile of towers and roadways, clustered around a protrusion in a range of cliffs overlooking one of Eurus's many scrubland plains.

It was the condition of the ruins that was their most immediate mystery. This small city had stood abandoned for two million years, wracked all that time by sun and storm, but most of the city's buildings looked only a few decades old. Among a sparse web of tumbled, indistinct wreckage that genuinely looked its age, many of the skyscrapers still gleamed in the daylight as if they were new. Whatever secrets lay behind the Sagittarians' auto-repair technology, their result was only too obvious. They had managed to hold off the ravages of time for untold millennia, and in the process had only deepened the mystery of why there was so little of their empire left.

The astroarchaeological exploration of this ancient complex hadn't been around quite as long as the complex itself, but it had been a fixture of Euran life almost as long as the planet had been inhabited by Humans. The plateau overlooking the city was the site of what was presumed to be a Sagittarian spaceport, and had been restored by the Commonwealth Academic Institute to serve much the same purpose in the modern day. All the ships supplying and supporting the archaeology effort came through this facility. But on this particular day, the port was especially busy. It was the beginning of Eurus's notorious dust storm season and meteorologists were forecasting that a particularly nasty one was brewing to kick things off. The Sagittarian city would ultimately barely notice the storm, but the scientists knew their equipment was not quite so hardy and were packing up to evacuate before it set in. The southern horizon was already obscured in a yellowish haze that would all too soon sweep over the site.

Professor Lorentz Kellermann had been a member of the first research team to re-enter the complex after the fury of the Interregnum had ended and life in this part of the Galaxy had returned to normal. He had been a constant part of the explorations ever since then, feeding a lifelong passion for astroarchaeology, and thus he had been a natural choice for the post of project director. At this point in time, it meant that he was standing in the centre of the spaceport, overseeing the last few personnel packing equipment into shuttles. Kellermann usually prided himself on ensuring things ran smoothly - indeed, in years prior all personnel and equipment would already be on the Academic Institute's orbital outpost well ahead of the season's first storms - but between the unexpected severity of the weather and a recent influx of additional gear, there was a lot more to be seen to this year. They had even had to leave some of it behind in the complex, secured as best they could manage, and just hope it would weather the storm.

Professor Kellermann looked up from the his datapad and soon regretted it, blinking furiously behind one hand to clear the dust out of his eyes. He pulled his goggles down over them and made his way over to the main cargo lift on the cliff's edge. A pair of research assistants had arrived on it and were pushing a hover-lifter before them, piled with crates and boxes. Kellermann didn't know who exactly they were - even if they weren't wearing the shapeless one-size-fits-all environmental suits, he wasn't much good with names and faces.

"Would this be the last of the equipment from Tower D-15?" he said to one of the suited scientists, shouting to be heard over the ever-loudening wind.

"Yes, Professor," came the reply from behind the blacked-out visor, "this should be everything."

"Excellent. Get it onto the shuttle, then!" Kellermann waved the lifter on, before something occurred to him and he stopped the scientist again. "What about Artifact 93?"

The scientist shook their head. "I'm sorry Professor, but there's no time to get it up here. Biren's team locked it down before they left, so it should be fine."

Kellermann grimaced to himself. Artifact 93 was a remarkable find, and not something he was comfortable leaving behind. Before he could say anything more about it however, yet another suited figure approached him.

"We've still got a little room in the shuttle, Professor. We're heading into the city for one last sweep - maybe we can pick the artifact up on the way?"

"One last sweep? No no, young woman, there's hardly enough time," Kellermann said. "We really ought to be leaving now, before the storm hits."

"Are you sure, sir?" asked another person. "Artifact 93 is pretty important, we should make sure it's properly secured. We'll stay with it 'til the storm dies down."

"He may have a point, Professor," one of the hover-lifter's crew said. "Olnyre's team is hunkering down in District A to keep an eye on things there. These two should be safe inside the main vault, and the storm will calm down in a few hours. We can send a shuttle to retrieve them then."

Kellermann nodded firmly. "Right. You two head down to the vault and make sure everything is properly sealed. Take my personal key, it should grant you full access."

The pair accepted Kellermann's key and hurried off to the lift, as the rest followed the hover-lifter into the shuttle. Once the cargo ramp retracted and the doors sealed, the ship took off and began to climb, but its flight was unsteady in the building winds. Before much longer, conditions would be impassable to anything less than the sturdiest ships.

The lift slowly descended down the cliff's face, giving its passengers a brief measure of shelter against the wind. The main vault was set into the cliff about a third of the way down - a massive door several metres high and wide, in a tunnel that had been revealed aeons ago by the collapse of part of the cliff face. A gantry had been built against the tunnel's edge to allow access from the lift. The scientists hurried across it, and the taller of the two fumbled with a nearby console. Although much of Sagittarian technology and culture was inscrutable to modern species, the research teams had made some progress into restoring some of the simpler systems. The vault door was one of them, and at the console's command the hefty round panel slid ponderously aside. The pair of scientists hurried through the doorway, and the door ground shut again after them. The tunnel rang with its hollow boom, and was left in darkness.

Ancient lights flickered into life after a second or two, casting a cold and barely adequate illumination over a complex that seemed to have shut out the rest of the world altogether. Even now, the noise of the storm was barely a low rumble outside the door, as if even the fury of the elements was afraid to make itself known here. Not quite so intimidated, one of the two scientists set about pulling off their helmet. He hung it behind his back and looked around at his surroundings.

"What a lovely place this is," Laszlo Hadron muttered to himself. The quiet sarcastic remark echoed away into the shadowed depths of the complex, bouncing off the grey, millennia-old walls like an unwelcome cough in a dead-quiet library. Laszlo had the vague impression that their presence was an intrusion, that these dusty catacombs did not want him here. He couldn't help but shiver at the notion, but it didn't stop him from walking into the central chamber before him.

A huge round space had been carved into the rock, ringed with wide balconies at regular intervals. Set into the walls of the upper levels were openings to wide cavernous spaces, and the lower levels were filled with smaller and more numerous alcoves, connected here and there with walkways in varying states of disrepair and decay. Gazing around at all this, Laszlo suddenly realised what he was looking at. As if he were staring at an optical illusion and his eyes had just shifted focus, his perception of the chamber flipped radically. What at first glance had seemed to be nothing more than old ruins he now recognised as the concourse of a spaceport.

As Laszlo imagined the ancient space filled with the people who long ago might have used it, Isis joined him near the edge of the central shaft. As she pulled her crimson ponytail out of the neck of her suit, she idly flexed her pointed ears - the enviro-suit's helmet had been a bit too cramped for them to fit comfortably. The black sphere given to them by Mat followed by her side, hovering at about shoulder level, a blue light glowing softly on the front as though it were some sort of eyeball.

"Quite a fascinating locale, isn't it?" the sphere said in a hushed voice. It was Mat's voice, though it sounded a little less impressive coming from a sphere the size of a tennis ball rather than a star-sized one.

"Mmm," Laszlo said in agreement, not looking away from the concourse. "I'm guessing that all this was the city's main spaceport once upon a time?"

"Indeed it was. Part of it, anyway." Mat's remote eye tilted up to look at the top of the shaft, which was sealed with an iris door. "Directly above us would have been the external landing pads - and indeed they are that again today, thanks to the Commonwealth Academic Institute."

"How long has the CAI been here?" Isis asked.

"Approximately 315 Commonwealth standard years, give or take a week or so," Mat said. "These ruins were the primary reason for Eurus's colonisation, in fact. Humanity had never before seen anything like this."

"Well..." Laszlo said thoughtfully, cocking his head to listen to the faint rumble of the storm, "I don't think we have quite that long. Didn't that professor mention an "Artifact 93" or something?"

Isis brought up a computer tablet. "Yep. That might be what we're here for - the local map says it's in a chamber just off Hangar F-3. This way..."

The trio turned away from the railing and made their way deeper in the spaceport catacombs. They passed several hangars on the way down to the shaft's bottom, each of them a yawning empty chasm. The still, silent darkness framed by each one was somehow more unnerving than any conceivable alternative. Piles of crates, an ancient starship, even a mound of skeletons... any might at least have been a sign that there had once been life in this place. But whether time had simply worn it all away or whether the city had been deliberately abandoned, there was nothing like that here. There was a very distinct emptiness here that seemed to transcend the mere absence of things.

Hangar F-3 was not quite as empty as the other hangars around the ring, but not with any remnant of the Sagittarians. The excavation teams had moved a lot of equipment in, having apparently centred their explorations of the spaceport interior there. Following a power cable from a portable fusion generator, the three entered an aperture that had been cut into the hangar wall, where an ancient door had been carefully removed and put to one side. Inside the doorway was a series of rooms, roughly carved out of the rock and metal with none of the care or effort with which the rest of the spaceport had been constructed. The few articles of furniture and pieces of equipment still surviving in any recognisable shape were similarly spartan and undecorated, pure function with no consideration for style.

Isis looked around at the plain, near-cubic room, somewhat unimpressed. "What was this for?"

"It's not really clear," Mat replied, as they hovered in behind her, "but by all indications they are somewhat more recent than the rest of the complex. It's theorised they were created during the Extinction itself."

Laszlo poked at ancient consoles, eventually moving to a free-standing Commonwealth one. It was wired into a sturdy metal door in the wall, and as Laszlo toyed with the buttons it ground heavily outward, to reveal another chamber wreathed in shadow. Laszlo pressed another button and the lights flickered into life.

"Aahh... that must be the famous Artifact 93 we've heard so much about."

In the centre of the chamber was a raised plinth, upon which rested a large wedge of ancient metal. It appeared to have been broken off from a circular unit, as the straight edges were scorched and scored irregularly, and densely layered with strata of circuitry and computer hardware.

Isis and Laszlo both bent over the artifact to examine it closely, and even Mat hovered low over the object, eye-light focused squarely on its surface.

"So this is what all the fuss is about?" Laszlo said in a hushed whisper.

"Yes, this it it. I've been decoding more of the datacell, and Artifact 93 is described quite explicitly," Mat answered. "There can be no doubt that we've found what we're looking for."

"So, what actually is it?" Isis asked.

"As to that, I'm afraid I can't tell you. Deep penetrating scans indicate that it is filled with computer circuitry, and it appears designed to interface with something. But what that may be is completely unknown."

"What does these symbols say?" Isis asked, gesturing to Sagittarian text inscribed along the curved outer edge. "Maybe they give some sort of clue."

Mat's eye-light flitted back and forth across the text. "It's difficult to say, alas. The Sagittarian language is very dissimilar to most modern languages, and it doesn't help that this inscription appears to be incomplete. But their best guess indicates that this says "The Wargod lies within its tomb"."

Laszlo arched an eyebrow. "Well, that sounds ominous."

"Indeed," Mat agreed, floating back up to eye level. "But perhaps more clues may become apparent if we were to acquire the other pieces."

"There's more of this thing, eh?"

"Indeed so. At least three pieces, by the Commonwealth's best guess. One of them is currently being stored in a secret Department of

Operations facility. I'll have decoded its coordinates by the time you've returned to the Wyvern."

Laszlo and Isis straightened up together, all business once more. "Then let's get this thing out of here," Isis said. She worked her arms under the bulk of the artifact and hefted it off the plinth. "Nngh! I'll get this thing packed up, and you call in the Wyvern, Las."

"On it!" Laszlo fished a small computer panel out of a pocket in his suit and began tapping at it as he followed Isis out of the chamber. In the hangar they found an empty crate big enough for the artifact and loaded it onto a hovercart, before retracing their steps back to the cliffside door.

Outside, the dust storm was blowing at full strength. Even muffled by the metre-thick door, the sound of it was almost deafening in the antechamber. Isis pushed the hovercart up to the door and looked up appraisingly at it. As she pulled her helmet back up and tucked her hair into her suit, Laszlo stepped up beside her, still working at his panel.

Isis turned her helmetted head to him. "Ready?"

Laszlo lowered the panel and put on his own helmet. "Ready."

With that, he stepped over to the console and opened the door. Immediately the chamber was filled with noise and dust. Laszlo felt like he was walking in tar as he groped his way back to Isis and the hovercart, battered by the wind. Together, the pair of them forced the hovercart out onto the lift platform, struggling to get it going where they wanted it. Neither of them could see more than a couple of metres in front of them, if even that far.

"I can't see a bloody thing!" Laszlo shouted. If it hadn't been for the radio in his suit, Isis wouldn't have heard him at all. "There's no point keeping the Wyvern cloaked in this. Hang on..."

He jabbed the computer panel hanging from his hip, and at the command there was a haze of light before them. As it faded, it left behind the stern of the Wyvern, the now-uncloaked ship holding position just before the platform. Freed of the light-bending field, the nacelles were burning brightly to keep it in place, and the cargo bay's interior was an island of serenity and clear visibility before them, sheltered by the hull of the ship. The pair of pirates hurried up the entry ramp before them, pushing the crate into the relative calm of the cargo bay. As he stepped onto the deck plating, Laszlo released the crate and hurried to close the doors.

"Lovely weather we're having..." he muttered sarcastically, pulling his helmet off and looking around at the drifts of dust that had blown in. Isis ignored his grousing and pulled off both her own helmet and the lid of the crate. Out from inside it floated Mat.

"Back on your ship, I take it? Marvellous, nicely done!" he said by way of greeting.

"Thanks, Mat," Isis answered, "So, where to next? You did say you'd have decoded the coordinates by now."

"Indeed I have. Bring me to the navigation computer and I'll mark out our course."

*   *   *

Given its interstellar range of operations, it was only natural that the Commonwealth Academic Institute would have its own dedicated space fleet, but it often surprised people to learn that the Scientific Expeditionary Fleet was the third largest in the Commonwealth. It was almost as large a navy as the Galactic Survey's fleets of scout ships, though the Solar Navy easily outweighed both of them combined. The elegant, curved forms of the CAI's science ships were a common sight throughout the Commonwealth, and the SEF even maintained a private network of space stations for its own use. One such station was over Eurus, trailing a few hundred kilometres behind the planet's main surface/orbital port facility. At its current point in its orbit it afforded a wonderful view of the area around the Sagittarian city, and on a clear day one could even have picked out the glimmering speck that was the city itself. But with the storm season set to continue for the next few months, it was now hidden beneath ragged-egded waves of cloud cover, stained a dirty yellow by all the loose dust and sand they carried. There would be no access to the city until the storms calmed down, and no real scientific work would be possible for the duration of the season, so most Institute personnel had withdrawn to the science station.

Professor Kellermann gazed idly out of his office's window down at the planet's tumultuous weather. Almost every year for most of his life, he'd been in the ruins uncovering the history of its ancient inhabitants. He was usually the last to leave when the storm season forced everyone out, and he was always the first to return to the site when it was safe to do so. He'd all but dedicated his life to the city's excavation, and the few months he spent outside it was primarily spent waiting patiently to return. Lost in idle thoughts, he eventually sighed to himself and brought his attention back to his paperwork. Although he was a dutiful member of the Academic Institute, he'd far prefer to have still been working on Artifact 93...

The sudden buzz of his intercom brought Kellermann out of his languid state of mind. He reached a hand forward to answer it.

"Yes, what is it?"

"Someone to see you, Professor," his receptionist replied. "They say it's quite important."

"Oh, well, send them in." Kellermann saved and set aside his work and straightened a few things on his desk, as the door opened and the visitor walked in. Kellermann was never very good with faces, but even aside from that he'd have been hard-pressed to describe them if asked after the fact, beyond their species and their plain grey-toned uniform. It was as if they had been designed to be unremarkable.

"Good afternoon, Professor Kellermann. Thank you for allowing me some of your time," they said in a polite, level tone. "I trust I'm not interrupting anything important?"

"Nothing that can't wait, not to worry. Please, take a seat." Kellermann gestured vaguely towards the chairs on the other side of his desk, one of which the visitor accepted and perched carefully in. "How can I help you?"

"I'm with the Department of Operations, Professor, and we understand that you've recently uncovered a certain unusual artifact?"

"Artifact 93? Yes, it's quite a fascinating piece, really..." For a moment, Kellermann started to mentally arrange a lecture on the subject, before catching himself. "Eh, but I'm sure you have other concerns. What interests you about it?"

"I'm sure I needn't tell you that Artifact 93 is thought to be connected to the Sagittarian Extinction. It's that which concerns us."

Kellerman's brow furrowed. "Well, that's our current understanding, but... the Extinction? Why should that be such a concern to the Department of Operations?"

"Let's just say that we'd rather not take any chances on the matter. Where is the Artifact now?"

"It's in its vault in the city at present. But I'm afraid you won't be able to see it at present. The dust storms prevent all access to the site, and they're not going to clear up any for at least the rest of the day."

"I realise that, Professor Kellermann," the agent continued in the same calm voice, "but the situation is at a critical juncture. It is very important that the Department is able to ascertain the Artifact's safety."

Kellermann bridled at the agent's insistence. "This isn't Earth, my young friend!" he said indignantly. "There are no climate machines here - I can't just turn off the weather for you!" He stopped and took a breath to steady himself, while the agent regarded him with the same politely neutral expression.

"However, I can show you the security camera uplink to the site," he continued, turning to his computer and opening the link. "We're still connected to groundside systems, even through the storm, so this should be enough to assuage your--"

Kellermann stopped with a little gasp, eyes widening with horror. The agent stood up and stepped around his desk to see the camera feed for themselves. The image of the screen was of a stone room with a pedestal in the centre - an empty pedestal.

The agent's hand shot to their earpiece in an instant. "Computer, scan for engine traces leaving the primary excavation site. Cross-reference with Academic Institute shuttle logs and report anomalies."

The computer of the agent's ship took only a moment to calculate the request. "Most recent unscheduled launch approximately thirty-four minutes and thirty-three seconds ago. Ionic trace begins at primary excavation site and terminates in high orbit. No ship detected."

The agent's face hardened just a little, but they remained all business. "Computer, run a full sensor sweep on the termination point.

Look for any trace of FTL jumps." They switched communications channel. "Secondary Vector CE362 to mission control, Objective Gamma has been compromised. Chasing one trace now."

If Kellermann had heard this, he didn't respond to it. He simply sat staring aghast at the screen showing the empty pedestal, and only looked away when the agent cleared their throat.

"Thank you for your assistance in this matter, Professor," they said, returning to their level tone. "But the situation now obligates me to take my leave."

"B-b-but, what about-- the Artifact... you will find it, won't you?" Kellermann stammered.

"We will keep you updated on the situation," the agent assured him smoothly, "as information security policies allow. For now, please remain calm. The Department is taking over."

Chapter 3

Sel'Akis was a place that had been left behind by history. In the earliest days of the Imperial Wars, in which Humanity had established a place of dominance in the Galaxy over the other major cultures neighbouring it, this strategically-placed planetoid had been a key staging point against the Syohar. But that was two hundred years ago, and the Galaxy had changed. The desperately belligerent Empire had been replaced by the more peaceable Commonwealth, the Syohar living in the sector had migrated to their peoples' new homeworld, and the remote Sel'Akis had lost relevance. The debris fields in its orbit had been picked clean of everything of historical interest and the military bases on its surface had been long dormant. They were not totally abandoned, however. Such a quiet and unregarded place was perfect for keeping things away from prying eyes, and the Department of Operations had capitalised on it. Antique facilities that had once been hangars and repair bays now served as storage vaults for a number of things that the Commonwealth preferred to keep quiet. The entire complex had been refitted to be fully automated, with no need for living personnel who might choose to reveal some of the Commonwealth's best-kept secrets.

This was what Mat had described to Laszlo and Isis as the Wyvern had made the jump from Eurus to Sel'Akis. The pirate vessel was now hiding in orbit over the planetoid, landed in a hole in the pipework of an old fuel depot, while the two prepared to infiltrate the base. They'd agreed that Isis was to be the only one to head down to the base proper, she and her equipment being far better suited to the stealth it would require, and Laszlo's familiarity with Commonwealth military design would only go so far. To that end, she had suited herself up in a full-body outfit that possessed similar technology to that which the Wyvern used to become invisible. In the briefing room overlooking the Wyvern's cargo bay, Isis made one last check of the weapons and equipment stowed magnetically to her stealthsuit, as Laszlo and Mat pored over a rough map of the facility.

"Unfortunately we can't really get a perfect idea of the base's layout from here - the depot's hull blocks our sensors as well as the base's," Laszlo explained, studying the hologram intently. "Might be able to get a closer look when we make the sweep, but I don't want to put out too much EM radiation. Anything more than a communications link and we risk detection."

Isis clipped a few spare magazines to her belt and stowed her rifle on her back. "I'm sure I can make do. Any idea what I'm up against?"

"Very little, I'm afraid," Mat said. "The facility is entirely automated, so there are no life readings we might otherwise use to make a guess. A comprehensive turret system would be a reasonable expectation, however. Combat robots are not also out of the question - I feel that avoiding a fight altogether may be the wisest plan."

"It usually is, but knowing our luck..." Isis shrugged. "Anyway, the artifact itself. What am I looking for?"

"The Department of Operations has given this artifact the designation A25-279D, so you'll need to keep an eye out for that. Certainly they're unlikely to have left it on a table for you to simply pick up."

"And they'll have probably realised by now that the first artifact is missing, so they may well be securing it," Laszlo added. "Just in case this wasn't going to be enough of a challenge for you."

Isis gave a little scoff. "Infiltrating a top-secret Department facility on the edge of the Commonwealth? Why ever would that be a challenge?" She pulled the hood of her suit up and worked her ears into their pockets. "But I think that's everything I need to start with. Let's get this done."

Laszlo nodded and turned off the map hologram. "Sounds good to me! No time like the present." He hurried up the stairs to the cockpit followed by Mat, while Isis walked down into the cargo bay. As she crossed the bay to the main doors, she felt the gentle rocking of the deck as the Wyvern took off.

In the darkness of the disused fuel pipe, the pirate vessel pulled up its landing gear and wobbled on its centre of gravity as manouevring jets held it steady. A measured impulse from its nacelles brought it gliding gently up out of the pipe - the ship and its engine flares were both invisible, but Laszlo wasn't taking any chances with excess emissions.

Laszlo looked out at space from the comfort of the pilot's seat. As the ship turned to face the planetoid, he mentally ran through the figures he needed. He could just as easily have had the navigation computers calculate the necessary course, but he'd been trained on such things since childhood. It was almost reflex to him by this point, and it was by pure instinct that he set the Wyvern on its path towards Sel'Akis.

"Making descent now, Isis. Get ready." Isis moved to the cargo bay control panel, pressing a few buttons to drain the air from the entire room. Safe in her environmentally sealed stealthsuit, Isis waited patiently as the sounds of the ship died out, indicating the transition to vacuum. Isis reached for a switch on a device on her belt as she crossed the room again, and at its activation her form was engulfed in a brief shifting aura of white light, that left seemingly nothing behind as it faded. The controls for the airlock doors were pressed by invisible fingers, and both sets slid open to reveal the landscape of Sel'Akis.

"6,000 metres from surface, drop point coming up."

The planetoid's craggy brown surface was coming up steadily as the Wyvern's course dipped down to its periapsis.

"2,000 metres."

Isis stood against the wall of the bay, staring fixedly out through the two sets of open doors, keeping her breathing steady.

"Approaching 500 metres."

Isis poised herself on her toes.

"Three... two... one..."

She shot forward into a sprint.

"Now!"

She jumped.

There was no sense of motion out in the void, beyond what one could see nearby. If Isis closed her eyes, it seemed as though she was still and alone in a sea of nothingness. She kept her eyes open, though, looking down at Sel'Akis' surface to gauge distance and speed. Even for as quick as she was on her feet, her jump hadn't slowed her down much from the Wyvern's orbital dive. The dusty rock rushed past her in a blur even as it drew ever closer to her, and she curled up into a protective ball. Milliseconds before she hit the ground, the shield projectors in her suit sent out a pulse of energy. A brief sphere flashed around her and absorbed the impact, slowing her down greatly and sending her tumbling back up from the ground. Isis uncurled herself for her landing. Her hands and feet drew long furrows in the dust as she hit the ground and skidded to a halt.

Isis straightened up, dusted herself off, and put her hand to her earpiece. "Isis to Wyvern, landfall made. Ready to proceed."

"Good. I'm heading back around the planetoid - I'll set her back down in the fuel orbital. Shall I send you the ground sweep?"

"Go ahead."

A notification of a data download appeared in Isis' visor, and she called it up. A relief map of the area she was in resolved itself before her eyes. Red lines superimposed on it indicated artificial construction - the base itself.

"Looks like there's a small entrance in this fissure here, a kilometre away from your position," Laszlo said, as a hand-drawn circle drew itself on Isis' map. "Probably an old maintenance access hatch. That'll be your best bet for a way in."

"Got it. Heading there now." She looked out over Sel'Akis' surface, and kicked off gently into the characteristic long bounce of low-gravity walking.

"Any sign of heightened security yet? They must have found out about the missing artifact on Eurus by now."

"Can't really tell, I'm on low-emissions. If there is anything out there, it's on the other side of the--" Laszlo stopped as the sensors showed him something. "Wait... a ship just jumped in. It's making an orbital insertion now... I think it's Solar Navy."

"They must be here for A25-279D as well. I guess they've found out on Eurus after all," Isis surmised.

"D'you think we should abort the op?"

"No, I can work with this." Isis came to a graceful halt on the edge of the fissure, and forward to look inside. There was the doorway, set into the rock wall of the fissure's widest point, its status lights glowing a soft green. Isis hopped down off the fissure's lip and drifted down onto the platform before it. On the way down, she primed her custom hacking programs. Loaded onto a neural implant, she could control them with a mere thought, and low-level security systems didn't even need her direct input. Bolstered by a connection to the Wyvern's own digital countermeasures suite, Isis was confident that they could see her through whatever the base might throw at her.

She thought her way through the airlock's security, and pressed the access button. Somewhat to her surprise, the status lights didn't pulse please-wait orange as she was expecting, but went straight to access-granted blue. She pushed the door aside and entered the airlock, and as the outer door slid shut behind her the inner door opened into the corridor without protest. Curious, she called up an environmental scan, and the readout confirmed her suspicions: the entire facility was in airless vacuum. The Department really wasn't expecting visitors.

As Isis investigated her surroundings, two security drones came racing around the corner to check out the unauthorised airlock access - a pair of gunbots, hovering at head level and moving fast. Isis glanced up at their motion signatures on her suit's sensors, and ducked unconcernedly under them as they rushed past her. She recognised their particular model, and knew they wouldn't be able to see through her cloak. True to her expectation, the two drones ignored Isis completely and began patrolling the corridor, searching for the intruder.

Isis gave the drones an appraising look, as she carefully probed their memory systems with her neural rig for any clues as to the artifact's location. Physically, the gunbots were little more than a turret sandwiched between modules housing engines, sensors and other systems. It was a simple and inexpensive design to build and maintain that could easily be lethal, but they were none too bright and not difficult to fool. She pulled out of the gunbot's memory and continued down the corridor. There had been nothing useful in the gunbots' memory drives, but they had alerted security to the unknown intruder.

The gunbots were not the only security measure. Turrets were mounted at the corners where corridors met. They were fixed to point in one direction, rather than sweeping from side to side. Part of Isis couldn't help but grudgingly approve of this choice -she had seen a lot of security systems, and all too many of them left gaps like that for intruders like her to exploit. If not for the fact that Isis's stealthsuit has rendered her invisible, she would have been unable to proceed unseen. Luckily she was invisible, and the turrets gave her no trouble.

What might have proved more troublesome, however, was what she came across next. As she made her way down a corridor into what had been the base's habitation deck, she saw a humanoid security robot on patrol. She was shocked by the sight - the Interregnum had only ended just over thirty years ago, and the memory of robotic armies marching on helpless Imperial worlds, destroying and conquering, was still fresh in Humanity's cultural memory. Public opinion of military machinery with any degree of autonomy was less than positive to say the least, and a lot of the Commonwealth had eschewed all but the most benign and closely supervised automation. What would drive the Department to resort to this?

As Isis stared at the robot, the robot was also staring in her direction. She didn't notice until it raised its gun. Seeing the weapon pointing at her was enough to shake her out of her surprise, and she readied her own weapon. Neither of them took the shot as the robot studied the corridor before it. Something about it seemed confused. It may have detected a faint trace that Isis's cloaking device couldn't quite cover up, but her hacking programs were aggressively jamming all the systems it could affect and the robot was unable to process what it saw or contact its mainframe for help.

Isis didn't feel like waiting for the robot to figure things out and opened fire. The robot staggered back and shot back in the direction of Isis's shots. Isis dove to the floor, narrowly avoiding the brunt of the robot's gunfire. The two traded shots, until finally the robot slumped and collapsed, its armour perforated and its systems sparking. Isis rose to her feet, keeping her gun trained on the downed machine as she stalked towards it. She gave it a shove with her foot, but it seemed dead. She couldn't rest on her laurels, though - even with the alarm systems jammed it wouldn't be long before something noticed the lack of updates from this robot and came to investigate. Isis hurried past the remains of the robot and through the door it was guarding.

The room inside looked like the control centre. In the middle was a large console with a holoprojector, and smaller consoles lined the room's walls. All of this was set under a transparent dome, which seemed to have been a common feature of Human space facilities for centuries. Isis didn't stop to admire the view though, since she was more interested in the central console. One of its terminals had been replaced with a modern system. She stepped over to it and pressed a few buttons. Hacking her way past its security, she found a directory listing hundreds of items. Each one was titled with a serial number much like the one Mat had told her to look for.

"Isis to Wyvern. I'm looking up the artifact in the base computer. Any more word on the Navy ship?"

"It's taken up orbit of the planetoid," came Laszlo's reply, "and it just launched another ship. Looks like you might have company shortly. Three minutes 'til it lands, at the most."

"Shit..." Isis muttered to herself as she entered the artifact's number into the computer. For several painfully long seconds, the database shuffled through itself... and eventually brought up the results she was after. She memorised its location on the base map and shut the system down. As the screen switched off though, she caught sight of something outside the dome. A shuttle glided silently above, en route to the hangars.

"Shit!" Isis repeated, and hustled out of the command centre at top speed.

*   *   *

Apart from the control room, the hangars were the only part of the base that protruded through the surface of Sel'Akis. Ordinarily the thick metal of the doors was difficult to distinguish from the planetoid's crust, scored by meteor impacts and littered with dust, but as the heavy door of the main hangar slid open to admit the shuttle, the light from the facility broke through the murk of deep space. The shuttlecraft was dwarfed by the cavernous bay as it descended into it and onto the pad in its centre. This part of the base had originally been built to handle the needs of freighters and frigates back when it was the main outpost of the Imperial war effort, and the similarly massive cargo bays radiating off it had been stocked to the ceiling with supplies going in and out at all hours. But today, the base was all but forgotten, and even the lone shuttle's visit was an unusual occurrence. What cargo was periodically delivered to the base was not intended to be used.

From some dark, quiet corner of the hangar, Isis watched as the shuttle touched down on the landing platform. As alarmed as she'd been at its arrival, its presence actually answered quite a few questions for her. For starters, how would she get to the artifact itself? The cargo bay doors were a bit too big for her to open on her own. But now she didn't have to worry about that, as the base's systems opened them automatically, doubtless already appraised of the shuttle's mission. As a lifter drone floated into the dark cargo bay, Isis jumped down from her perch and made her way onto the platform. She glanced through the ship's windscreen into the cockpit as she walked past it. Thanks to her stealthsuit, the two Naval personnel crewing it wouldn't have seen her even if they had chanced to look up. Isis couldn't make out any markings that might have told her which ship they served on, but she at least was able to determine their armament. She loosened something in its holster as she approached the loading ramp at the back of the ship.

The second question the shuttle answered for her: how would she have gotten the artifact out of Sel'Akis when she had found it? Trying to bring the Wyvern in would have been far too risky, and if the artifact itself was the same shape as its Euran counterpart it would have been a bit too awkward to simply carry. But with this shuttle, flying it out was no problem at all for Isis - she wouldn't be much of a pirate if she couldn't steal a ship - and the Wyvern could always use an extra shuttle.

The lifter drone drifted back over to the landing pad, a large crate of distinct plainness clutched in its grabbers. As the robot lowered the crate to the level of the shuttle, Isis stepped up to peer at the number printed on the side: "A25-279D". That was it! As the shuttle's loading ramp unfolded and the lifter drone began to load the crate, Isis stepped smartly up into the shuttle and found a quiet corner to crouch down in.

The shuttle's two-person crew had no idea that they were taking on passengers as well as cargo. All they could see on the rear compartment's camera feed was the crate, and the quickly departing limbs of the lifter drone. As they slipped from view, the loading ramp automatically started to close and seal. The gentle hollow thud of its closing was followed by the low hiss of the compartment repressurising.

"Cargo loaded," the pilot reported, "requesting departure permission."

"Permission granted, have a safe flight." the base's computer replied.

The pilot closed the channel, and opened another. "Shuttle One to bridge. The cargo is loaded and we're heading back with it now."

"Acknowledged, Shuttle One. Come on back home."

The pilot closed the channel and lifted the shuttle back into open space. The ship turned to face its vector and headed off back to its mothership.

As it flew on, the co-pilot furrowed his brow at something amiss on his readouts. "Huh... there's a weight anomaly in the cargo bay. Did we take on anything other than that crate?"

"I wasn't told about any other cargo..." the pilot answered. She called up the readout and peered at it for a moment. Whatever the extra mass was, it was about the same mass as a person. But the Sel'Akis base was uncrewed, wasn't it?

A muted clunk rang through the compartment. It was the cargo-side airlock door - someone wanted to get in.

Both crewmembers stared at the airlock in wide-eyed terror, as every horror story they had ever read, seen and played paraded themselves unbidden across their imaginations. They exchanged a glance and, as the airlock repressurised itself, went for their sidearms. The door slid open and they took aim... but there was no-one there. There was only one thing out of place inside the antechamber, sitting in the middle of the floor...

A blinding flash and a deafening shriek filled the cockpit, and both crewmembers recoiled in pain from the stun grenade. Before either could begin to recover from the literal assault on their senses, each of them was seized and knocked out with an electric crackle. As they slumped unconscious in their seats, an invisible figure pulled them out and dragged them into the corner. The security camera overlooking the cockpit was the next victim, impaled on a combat knife.

Satisfied that she wasn't liable to be seen, Isis switched off her cloaking device. She stowed her knife and her stun prod and settled into the recently vacated pilot's seat. She took up the controls and began altering the shuttle's course.

"Shuttle One, you've changed course, what's the problem?" Isis glanced at the comm panel as it chimed in, before leaning over to switch it off. "Shuttle One, please respo--"

Isis shut down the shuttle's comm array, severing all connections to the outside. "They're not available right now, please leave a message," she muttered to herself. "Isis to Wyvern. I've secured the artifact aboard a transport shuttle. Heading to the rendezvous point now."

"Nicely done, Isis! See you at the rendezvous."

Isis set a new course for the shuttle as she talked to Laszlo. There weren't a lot of notable features in this star system besides Sel'Akis itself, and a long-abandoned surveillance satellite on the edge of the system was pretty much the only other thing most people would notice on the map. It was thus the natural choice for a rendezvous point, with the benefit of being easier to find than a set of random coordinates in empty space.

She engaged the shuttle's FTL drive, and leaned back in the seat for just a moment. The journey across the system's radius was only a short distance in terms of lightspeed - barely a few hundred million miles - and even the shuttle's low-powered drive could manage it in less than a minute. As she stretched and yawned, Isis barely paid any attention to the superluminal smear of electromagnetic frequencies outside, before the shuttle slowed back down to normal speeds within sight of the satellite.

As she brought the shuttle in alongside the satellite, Isis peered at the sensor readings from the immediate area. She was mystified by what she saw: the satellite had been abandoned and forgotten since the Imperial Wars, likely never used for centuries, yet it was giving off power readings. It wasn't a Navy power signature either, modern or antique, but something erratic and unstable.

Isis frowned doubtfully. "Are you there, Las?"

"Right here, Isis. Just pulling the Wyvern alongside you now," came Laszlo's reply. "What's up?"

"I'm getting power readings from the satellite, but I thought it had been abandoned. Are you getting anything on sensors?"

"No, sorry. I shut them down to avoid triggering the facility's detection grid, remember? Hang on, let them bring them up to low power..."

In the Wyvern's cockpit, Laszlo brought up its own sensors. It took a moment to fill in a map of the area, and gave Laszlo a proper computer-assisted look at the satellite. True to Isis's report, it did indeed bear a small but distinct power signature. Laszlo furrowed his brow and had the sensors look more closely - even on low power, they could still see more than the shuttle's - hoping to determine exactly what systems that power was feeding. He studied the results for a moment, and found them familiar. He'd seen them before... he knew what they were.

"Ohh, fu--"

Everything went dead. Before Laszlo could process it, the power readings surged and every light and sound died away. Laszlo was left sitting in the darkness of the Wyvern's cockpit, staring blindly at the blank screen. As he turned on the headlights of his suit, he slumped back into his chair with a sigh of utter frustration. An EMP mine was a beginner ploy, and he should have seen it coming even without sensors. Especially in this particular arrangement, since he'd used them many times back when...

Outside the Wyvern's cockpit window, an FTL flash briefly provided the only real illumination to be seen. In its wake was a ship that Laszlo knew all too well.

It was the Corsair. And that meant Morgan Strannik.

Chapter 4

The Corsair was an old ship. Even when the Interregnum began over sixty years ago, it had been serving in the Solar Navy for a number of years, and the war had not been kind to it. Serving as a Privateer vessel since then was a rough life for any vessel, and the Corsair's hull bore its share of scars.

For all his history with the old vessel, Laszlo should have been happy to see it, even if he weren't dead in space and in dire need of rescue. Serving on the venerable ship had been the beginning of his pirate career, and he'd even served as its captain after the retirement of his mentor, Ealonn Haque. However, this appointment had been over the objections of first mate Morgan Strannik, and he had never really accepted the young Hadron as his captain. In the end, it had led to Strannik leading a mutiny against him, and attempting to murder him in the process. Laszlo had never been fond of Morgan, and that eventful day had done little to endear Strannik to him.

In the darkness of the disabled Wyvern's cockpit, Laszlo stared sullenly at the Corsair as it flew into position under the Wyvern. If it weren't for the EM mine's field suppressing the ship's power, Laszlo would have been manning the guns, and taking great pleasure in doing so. As it was, alas, his resources were limited, and so too were his options He mentally ran through what he did have and came up with nothing useful. He didn't really feel like making a dramatic last stand in the cargo bay, nor did self-destructing the Wyvern out of spite particularly appeal to him.

As he was reaching these mental dead ends, there was a chime from the comm system. He leaned forward towards the screen, hoping that it might have been Isis, but he didn't recognise the frequency. Even so, he could hazard a guess as to who was calling. He considered blocking it, but he didn't really have anything else to do at the moment. In any case, it would be refreshing to have something specific to direct his frustration against.

The holographic picture was laggy and riddled with static through the EM field, but Laszlo would know that scarred, battle-worn face anywhere. Despite the toad-like smirk currently plastered across it, it was not a face that was frequently given over to smiling.

"Morgan, Morgan, Morgan..." Laszlo said by way of greeting, counterpointing Strannik's smug grin with a murderous scowl, "what a pleasure this isn't."

"Well, I for one am more than happy to see you like this, Las!" Morgan replied.

"You mean unable to fight back?"

Morgan shrugged, his smugness undaunted. "I'm a simple soul, of simple pleasures. Besides, who in our line of work doesn't enjoy an easy job?"

A series of hollow clunks came up to Laszlo from the lower reaches of the Wyvern. The Corsair had attached itself.

"Very good of you and Isis to go and get those Sagittarian artifacts for me, by the way - thanks so much." The smugness in Morgan's voice was by this point thick enough to leave a trail of slime in Laszlo's ears. "I'll be taking care of them now, though. Your services are no longer needed."

"What's your interest in those things anyway, Strannik?" Laszlo asked. "I never quite had you pegged as the astroarchaeological type."

"I've heard the legends too, y'know - a long-buried weapon that brought down an civilisation. A weapon that can end empires... or maybe buy them."

"So that's all you want? A bigger gun and a fatter wallet?"

"Right, 'cause I'm sure you've got much more noble ideas about them than I have," Morgan spat back, his smile hardening into his usual bitter glare. "You think you're so much better than me--"

"I don't THINK I am, Morgan," Laszlo said, his mouth curling into one of his favourite infuriating grins, "I KNOW I am."

Morgan glared, seething, at Laszlo for a moment, before speaking again. "D'you know what the difference between us is, Laszlo? Hmm? There is none, not really. You can prance around the Galaxy wearing some long-dead war hero's surname and that stupid cape--"

"-- it's a cloak, you idiot--"

"-- all you damn well please, but don't think you're not the same kind of asshole I am. I'm just honest to myself about it."

Morgan looked away from his camera at an unseen crewmember for a moment. He nodded at their report and jerked a thumb over his shoulder by way of command, then turned back to Laszlo.

"Anyway, I'd love to stay here and blow you up, but there's a Commonwealth destroyer on its way here, and we'd better make ourselves scarce. Maybe they'll do me a favour and execute you on the spot. It'd save me the trouble." His smirk returned one last time as he waved a patronising goodbye.

The picture cut out, leaving the Wyvern's cockpit once again in darkness, and there was another FTL flash as the Corsair jumped out of the system.

"What a lovely person..."

Isis's voice, fuzzy though it was through the EM field, was a welcome sound to Laszlo. "He's as charming as ever he was," Laszlo replied, as he fruitlessly tried to get a response from the ship. "Are you alright, Isis?"

"Still in one piece. They didn't even bother with me, they just took the artifact."

"Same over here. They left us alive, though, so we're not out of the game yet."

"Maybe not..." Isis answered, a tinge of doubt in her voice. "Are you getting any response from the Wyvern?"

Laszlo flicked the reactor ignition switch a few times, to no avail. "None whatsoever. Anything on your end?"

"Nothing, this shuttle's dead in the water." The faint sound of buttons and switches mirrored Laszlo's own attempts to get a response. "So... any thoughts about what to do about that destroyer?"

"None whatsoever. This is something of a pickle, eh?"

"Looks that way. Hard to see how things could get much worse..."

"Oh, I dunno. For all we know, that destroyer could be the Durendal, with my good friend Elgar on board." Laszlo chuckled ruefully at his own sarcasm. "It seems like it's a day for meeting old friends. Wouldn't that just be the cherry on top?"

At that moment, the destroyer in question jumped into the scene. As with all ships in the Solar Navy, it was the same basic shape: long and thin like the blade of some immense starborne sword, with specific variances in design as per a given class's function in battle. In the case of this destroyer, that meant two massive cannons mounted in the prow section either side of the centre, easily a third of the ship's length.

Isis studied the profile of the ship before them. "Isn't that a Greatsword-class?"

Laszlo was also examining the ship, and its form was unmistakable to his Navy-trained eyes. "... it can't be..."

Another comm frequency cut in on their conversation, not bothering with the niceties of awaiting approval.

"This is Captain Elgar Humboldt of the Commonwealth warship Durendal--"

"Oh bloody hell, I was JOKING!!"

"... wh--... th-- erm, that's... not the response I was expecting..." Captain Humboldt blinked, then cleared his throat and tried to regain his momentum. "In any event, you are both under arrest for the theft of Commonwealth property. You are ordered to stand down, disarm all weapons, and prepare to be taken into custody."

"That's not going to be difficult," Isis muttered. "Both our ships are disabled, if you hadn't noticed."

"I think you'll find that's OUR ship you're sitting in, Ms. Lagato - to say nothing of you, Hadron. Be that as it may, we'll be bringing both vessels into our hangar. Please lay down any weapons you may be carrying and await boarding."

Captain Humboldt terminated the link, and turned to his first officer. Leurak was busy with xir own duties, absorbed in holoscreens. Xe soon dismissed them once xe was done.

"Recovery ships are away, Captain, and marines are standing by in the hangar. I've also dispatched an engineering team to disable the EM mine on the satellite."

Humboldt nodded in approval. "Very good, Mx. Leurak. Make sure the brig has a couple of cells free for our newest... guests." Elgar couldn't help but smirk just a little, but he wrestled his face back into a veneer of professionalism. "I'd better update our passenger on the situation, he'll want to know."

He called up his own holoscreen and dialled in the frequency. The call was answered almost immediately.

"Yes, Captain?"

"We've apprehended Hadron and Lagato, Agent, although it seems someone else made off with the artifacts themselves."

"Very good, Captain. Please have an interrogation room prepared, I'd like to discuss the situation with them. And I'd like you to be in attendance as well, if you've no objections?"

"None at all, Agent. I'll see to it at once." The call ended, and Captain Humboldt called up another. "Captain to brig. Prepare an interrogation room for the incoming prisoners."

"Shall I assume I'll be taking care of things up here for now, Captain?" Leurak chimed in.

"Yes, Mx. Leurak, thank you," Humboldt replied as he dismissed his holoscreen. "Though I shouldn't think we'll have too much to do until we've decided what to do about the prisoners." At the mention of them, the smile returned to his face.

"You look pleased, sir," Leurak remarked with amusement.

"What can I say, Commander? It's a good day!"

*   *   *

As with most criminals, Laszlo and Isis both made it a general policy to avoid capture and incarceration like the plague. Alas, as today had proven, sometimes fate conspired to make the undesirable inevitable. Thus, having been all but dragged off the Wyvern by Navy marines, Laszlo had found himself being stripped of all his gear and left with nothing but a plain olive-drab jumpsuit and a pair of handcuffs. Neither were especially uncomfortable, but he felt naked without his customary spacesuit. It didn't help his mood at all.

As he trudged through the bowels of the Durendal, a pair of marines surrounding him all the while, he tried to formulate a plan of escape, if only to keep himself occupied. Unarmed and under guard as he was, his options were... limited, to say the least. And he still knew Elgar well enough to know that even for as tight a ship as he usually ran, security in the brig would really be on their toes for the duration of his and Isis's stay. For now, all Laszlo could think to do was to wait and see.

"In here." The lead marine had stopped suddenly in front of a door. They stood beside it as it opened and jerked their head room-ward at Laszlo.

Laszlo was a little perplexed, but he entered anyway. Inside the little room was a plain table bolted to the floor, with two chairs on either side of it. Sitting in one of them was...

"Hey, Las."

"Isis!" Laszlo broke into a grin and promptly took the seat next to her. "I'm glad you're still in one piece!"

"Likewise," Isis said, smiling back at Laszlo. "Any idea what they want with us, though? I'd've thought we'd be sent straight to the brig."

As if in answer to this, the door opened once more to admit two people. One was Captain Humboldt, who regarded the pair with imperious suspicion. The other was a rather unremarkable someone wearing a grey uniform, somewhat similar in design to Humboldt's but much plainer and without Naval markings. Their own gaze was much more polite and level than the Captain's.

Both took the seats opposite the two pirates. Captain Humboldt folded his arms on the table and stared the pair down, while the other sorted through the files on their datapad. Presently they cleared their throat.

"Good afternoon Mr. Hadron, Ms. Lagato. I'm Agent Secondary Vector CE362 with the Department of Operations. Captain Elgar

Humboldt I assume you are already familiar with - he has kindly agreed to oversee the proceedings."

Laszlo gave a smug grin and a friendly nod to the Captain, who simply glared back. Unconcerned by this, the agent continued.

"I'm sure you've guessed by now that this is of greater interest to the Commonwealth than a simple freighter hijacking." Their tone of voice was mild yet detached, almost cold. "But I wonder if you fully appreciate the situation you have involved yourselves in?

"What exactly is that?" Isis replied, her own voice hard and snappish. Laszlo simply leant back in his chair, silently studying the scene.

"Are either of you familiar with the Sagittarian Empire?"

"The mighty, ancient civilisation that built an ultimate weapon about two million years ago and promptly vanished?" Laszlo said, receiving a nod of confirmation. "Yeah, we've both been paying attention."

"I see. Well, are you also aware that the artifacts formerly in your... possession are thought to be directly connected to the extinction of that empire?"

"We'd heard something about that too," Laszlo continued guardedly. "How directly, exactly?"

"We don't know - precise information on the Sagittarians is sparse at best. But we'd rather not take any chances with this."

"Empire-destroying weapons aren't really the sort of thing the Commonwealth wants to unleash," Captain Humboldt added sardonically. "No doubt you can guess why."

"Quite so. As it is, your actions have introduced a considerable complication to a delicate situation..."

"Correct me if I'm wrong, but didn't someone besides us already know about this whole business?" Isis interjected. "How else did that datacell end up on the Durendal to begin with? Seems to me you didn't have this thing as tight as you wanted it to begin with."

"And now you're going to great lengths to explain the whole situation to us," Laszlo continued, folding his legs with feigned casualness, "when I know for a fact that the good Captain would just as soon hand me off to the police as look at me, if he could."

"And I can't imagine the Department of Operations would feel any need to get involved in a simple pirate arrest job either," said Isis, nodding at the plain-uniformed person's direction, who simply cocked an eyebrow in response. "So I reckon you want us for something more than just letting us know how badly we screwed up - am I close?" Both she and Laszlo each flashed a grin at the pair.

Captain Humboldt and the Department agent were silent for a moment. They exchanged a brief glance, then the agent continued.

"Not to let you become overconfident, but... yes. You're correct on all counts."

"Especially the "hand over to the police" part," muttered the Captain, before speaking up. "Not that we're planning on letting you chat to anyone, but understand that what we're telling you is under strictest secrecy. You don't breathe a word of this, is that clear?"

"Crystal."

"Fine. Well, we weren't lying to you when we said that the Commonwealth is concerned about the Sagittarian Extinction, but we may have understated a little."

"Indeed. Our concern is more than simple caution," the agent continued. "The exact circumstances surrounding it are still a mystery, but the broad strokes of the story are clear. The Sagittarians built a weapon of unparalleled power to fight a rival power, and over the course of a few standard years, a decade at the most, both their enemy and then they were systematically annihilated. Two nations comparable in size to the Solar Empire, all but completely wiped out."

"And as an epitaph to their civilisation, the survivors left behind something called, according to our best translation, the "Wargod's Tomb"," Captain Humboldt concluded. "Now, I don't know what that might have meant to the Sagittarians, but to me it means trouble."

"But that was two million years ago," Laszlo said, not overly perturbed by the pair's grim portents, "is it really such a worry today?"

Captain Humboldt fixed a hard stare upon him. "Laszlo, I have no idea what could destroy an interstellar empire so completely, and quite frankly I don't want to find out. And neither, I suspect, do any of the trillion or so people living in the Commonwealth."

"Not to mention the other nations neighbouring us," the agent concurred. "It may well be the case that whatever this "Wargod" might be, it poses no threat to us. Perhaps it died aeons ago, perhaps its so-called tomb is merely a monument to the bygone empire that built it. But whatever the case, the Commonwealth wants to know for sure, and to have the situation under control, whatever it may be."

"And with two Sagittarian artifacts in the hands of pirates, that's not really the case."

"And you're getting desperate enough that you're willing to... engage our services?" Laszlo asked, smirking just a little.

"Yes, we are," the agent concluded, a trace of a sigh entering their voice.

Laszlo and Isis exchanged a look, silently conferring. Isis nodded to Laszlo, and Laszlo nodded to Isis. They looked back.

"So what's the job?" Laszlo asked. "And what's the pay?"

Captain Humboldt looked as though Laszlo had just reached across the table and tweaked his nose. "Pay?" he spat. "You're asking to be paid for this?! What, is being kept out of prison not enough for you two?!"

"No," Laszlo said bluntly, "not if you're just planning to delay locking us up until we're of no further use to you." He leant back, regarding Humboldt with an arched eyebrow, almost daring him to argue. Humboldt glared back, his face the very picture of affronted disgust, but he had no answer.

The agent cut in with a clearing of their throat. "In light of the dire situation, I think perhaps an arrangement could be made. What would your price be?"

"Well, if we're going to be possibly saving the Galaxy from destruction," Isis said, "then shall we start the bidding at, say... a full pardon for our crimes?"

Humboldt scoffed in indignation. Even the agent's carefully neutral face was tinged with incredulity.

"That... may be difficult to sell to my superiors." The agent rubbed their chin in thought for a few seconds. Everyone awaited their next reply in expectant silence.

"Alright, here's what I propose: I might be able to negotiate for a provisional pardon. You'll enjoy the same benefits, on the condition that any further lawbreaking will reinstate your original criminal status. How does that sound?"

Laszlo and Isis exchanged glances once again. They were still silent, but their expressions said everything they needed to.

Laszlo looked back, grinning broadly. "Deal!"

Chapter 5

Elgar Humboldt was not having the best day. Even an hour after talking with Laszlo and Isis, his hackles were still raised. Rather than return to the bridge in a bad mood and risk taking his frustration out on his crew, he had instead decided to spend some time on the recreation deck to let himself unwind. Thus he sat slumped in a plush couch in the crew lounge, sipping something cool and fruity (and non-alcoholic) and gazing silently out into the characteristic quasi-luminescent haze of metaspace.

"Is this a private party, or can anyone join?"

Elgar looked up at the voice and found himself looking back into the otter-like face of Emara Larroe, the Durendal's chief engineer.

"Hello, Commander. Feel free to take a seat, I'm just thinking."

He shuffled to one side of the couch to make room for the Suura officer. She curled her tail to one side and sat down, crossing her legs and folding her hands on one knee. "About anything in particular?"

"Nah, not as such. Just... thinking, really." Elgar's eye was drawn idly to the glint of the polished metal panels of Larroe's cybernetic arms. His gaze lingered distractedly on them for a second, before he took another sip of his drink and resumed staring into metaspace.

Larroe was also looking at Elgar. She was regarding his expression appraisingly. "You look a bit troubled, Captain, if you don't mind my saying. Something about the mission?"

"Something like that. One of the prisoners... well, I have history with him."

"An old enemy?"

Elgar sighed a little. "Old friend, actually. Once upon a time."

"I guess this was before he did whatever it was that made him a wanted man?"

"Yes, naturally." Another sip of his drink. "We studied at Eurybia Naval Academy together, as it happens."

Larroe's interest was piqued. "Seriously? He was a Navy cadet?"

"Mm-hmm. My best friend, too. But we had a bit of a difference of opinion... his opinion being that it was a good plan to go AWOL a few months before our ensign exams, steal an SF20 Claymore and break a Privateer out of prison. I disagreed, of course, but I couldn't dissuade him."

"Wow... why'd he do something like that?"

"He had this romantic notion that the Privateers were the unsung heroes of the Interregnum who were unfairly maligned when the Commonwealth declared them a criminal organisation. That's as maybe, I told him, but you can't ignore the fact that many of them carved out the modern criminal underworld. He wouldn't have any of it, of course - he always was the impulsive type."

Larroe nodded eagerly, engrossed in the story. "Then what happened?"

"Well, he goes off to spring this Privateer from prison - someone called Haque, I think - and off they vanish into the black. Since I was the last person he spoke to before that, I was hauled in for questioning. One of the teachers seemed to think that I must have had something to do with the whole sorry business. He always had it out for me."

Elgar took another sip, and a few seconds staring sourly into the middle distance.

"Anyway, he did everything he could to ruin my chances of graduating, until the Lord Admiral himself stepped in and told him to knock it off. Still, needless to say, the whole experience left me a tad bitter."

"And now, we're doing dealings with that very same former friend that don't involve slinging him in jail where he belongs?" Larroe guessed.

Elgar gave her a sidelong glance, eyebrow cocked. "You'd heard about that, hmm?" he said in a low tone.

"I'd guessed about it, sir," Larroe answered with a shrug. "Engineering is a good place to keep an eye on the ripples - an ear to the ground, as you Humans say."

"Nothing gets by you, eh?" Elgar gave a wry smirk. "Well, the Department would probably rather we didn't talk about this, so let's keep it under our hats, shall we?"

Larroe grinned back. "My lips are sealed, sir!"

"Very good, Commander." Elgar glanced at his chronometer. "Well, I have a briefing to attend, so I'll have to take my leave of you now." He finished off his drink in one long swig, and stood up to leave.

"Thank you for listening, Commander. It was good to get that off my chest."

"Any time, Captain!" Larroe saluted her commanding officer. "It's always a pleasure. Enjoy the briefing, sir."

*   *   *

"Greetings, Agent CE362. We trust the situation is progressing smoothly?"

"Nothing has changed since last update, Administrators. Have you had a chance to consider Mr. Hadron and Ms. Lagato's proposal?"

In the specially shielded interior of the agent's ship, there was no real need for secrecy - no sensors could penetrate the compartment's bulkheads. Nonetheless, the holograms the agent was addressing were nothing more than anonymous vocal waveforms.

"We have, agent. A full pardon is quite a steep price, even a provisional one."

"Though Ms. Lagato is correct in saying that the safety of the Commonwealth is worth it."

"Do you believe they can be trusted?"

"I think so," the agent replied. "My impression of their character is a fundamentally honest one, criminal tendencies aside."

"And Captain Humboldt agrees with your assessment?"

"The Captain has no agenda here. He is not fond of Hadron, as I'm sure you are aware, but he is a Navy man through and through. He will set his prejudices aside for the good of the Commonwealth and its people."

"Very well, then. Proceed with the mission. We will make our own arrangements. Good luck, agent - Department out."

*   *   *

The Durendal's briefing room looked like a hybrid of a university lecture hall and an amphitheatre - a wide, descending semicircle of seating, divided in three blocks separated by stairs, arrayed before a holoprojector on a dais beneath a large wall-mounted screen. Usually intended for large groups of people, it was decidedly empty with only six people in it - Captain Humboldt, Agent CE362, Laszlo and Isis, and their two guards.

The two pirates, still in prisoners' jumpsuits, took their seats in the bottom row. Captain Humboldt and the agent were already waiting by the holoprojector.

"Thank you for joining us," the agent said by way of greeting.

"We didn't really have much else to do," Laszlo answered, shrugging dismissively. "Your brig isn't terribly fun, Captain."

"Well, I'm very sorry to hear that," Captain Humboldt muttered sarcastically back. "Anyway, I believe we can proceed with the briefing. Please go ahead, Agent."

"Thank you, Captain." The agent gestured towards the holoprojector, and images of the two Sagittarian artifacts appeared above it, side by side. "As I'm sure I don't need to tell you, before being apprehended by Morgan Strannik, Mr. Hadron and Ms. Lagato had already... acquired two of the Sagittarian artifacts."

The images of the artifacts turned in the air and arranged themselves as parts of a circle.

"What you both may have already intuited is that these artifacts are fragments of a larger whole, with a third completing the object. What you may not have known is that the location of the third artifact has been known to the Commonwealth for a few decades now."

Laszlo leant forward a little, brow furrowed. "It has? Why hadn't we heard about it?"

"Perhaps you hadn't decrypted that much of the datacell," Captain Humboldt murmured archly. He cleared his throat and resumed more professionally. "Anyway, this particular artifact was discovered thirty years ago, on the outskirts of the Inner Province. At the time, there was no real interest in the Sagittarians, and this was before any kind of reliable translation of Sagittarian language was possible. As such, It was regarded as nothing more than a curiosity."

"So what happened to it?" Isis asked.

"After the Academic Institute had studied it, it was purchased by a private collector in the Central Province, by the name of Areton Sarm," the agent explained. The image of the Sagittarian artifacts was replaced by one of a portly gentleman in expensive clothing. "Sarm is a major name in interstellar shipping and construction, having invested heavily in the reconnection efforts between the Central Province and the rest of the Commonwealth after the Interregnum. One of his major interests is astroarchaeology - he owns the largest private collection of historical artifacts in the Commonwealth. Naturally, that includes the third shard.

"The Academic Institute, and the Commonwealth itself, have both repeatedly attempted to purchase the shard from Sarm, but he has refused all offers. We don't know if he's aware of the situation surrounding it, but in any event he seems intent on keeping hold of it." The agent paused as they fixed their gaze on Laszlo and Isis. "Since legal attempts at its acquisition has failed us, we have no recourse but to resort to illegal ones."

"Ordinarily the Commonwealth wouldn't even consider this," Captain Humboldt interjected, "but we feel that averting a potential interstellar apocalypse is a somewhat greater priority than a Central Province bigwig's expensive hobby."

"Quite so, Captain," the agent said. "In short, we want the two of you to steal the Sagittarian artifact, without being detected."

"Fair enough," said Laszlo with a casual shrug.

"What's our latitude here?" asked Isis.

"We're willing to grant you whatever you feel you may require, in terms of both equipment and operational parameters," the agent explained. "We trust you to conduct this mission discreetly and with a minimum of fuss, and within those limitations you may feel free to structure the mission as you please. The Commonwealth will provide for your requirements."

"Good, we can work with that," Laszlo said. "In that case, we want all our stuff back. Including the Wyvern."

"Out of the question!"

Everyone's gaze snapped to Captain Humboldt in the wake of his sudden remark.

"Captain?" the agent said, raising their eyebrows queringly.

The Captain seemed to sense that he was outnumbered, but continued nonetheless. "That ship is a military prototype, which possesses stealth capabilities. How do we know you won't just use it to escape? We can't just hand over the keys just because you asked."

"Interstellar apocalypse, remember?" prompted Isis pointedly. "We need all our gear if we're going to get this done right, and that includes the Wyvern."

The agent moved to Humboldt's side. "Ms. Lagato has a point, Captain," they said, trying to soothe him. "Besides, one of the conditions of their provisional pardon is that the Wyvern be turned over to Naval custody as soon as the mission is concluded."

"They're right, Captain," Laszlo agreed, grinning, "we're only borrowing her for a bit!"

Captain Humboldt took a deep breath, glaring daggers at Laszlo's smug expression, before letting out a long quiet sigh. "Very well," he said, speaking barely above a sullen mutter. "I'll order the ship unlocked and prepared for launch. Will you be needing anything else?" There was more than a little sarcasm about the last sentence.

Isis ignored Humboldt's affront. "I think that's everything sorted out equipment-wise... all we really need now is to know where the artifact actually is."

"We don't have an exact location for you, Ms. Lagato," the agent answered, "the extent and expense of Sarm's collection is public knowledge, but its security isn't. However, we assume that it'll be on or near his estate in the city of Terratropolis."

"T-Terratropolis?" Laszlo asked in a hollow voice. He turned a little pale. "You mean, on Earth?"

"That's where the city was last time I checked," Captain Humboldt replied. Now it was his turn with the smug expression.

"Will that present a problem?" the agent asked, seemingly unaware of either Laszlo's fear or Humboldt's smugness.

"N-no, no, should still all be fine," answered Laszlo, not entirely unconvincingly. He swallowed, trying to still seem unconcerned. "Just out of curiosity, if we were to be caught by local law enforcement... ?"

"... then the Commonwealth would deny all involvement and you'd be on your own."

"Right. Thought you might."

"We'll burn that bridge if we come to it," Isis cut in. "For now, let's just concentrate on figuring out how we're going to approach this." She fell silent in thought for a moment.

"I think I've heard of Sarm before," Laszlo said, joining Isis in ponderance. "Old-school Central Province elite, isn't he? All money and entitlement?"

"That's one way you might put it," the agent said mildly, not quite disagreeing.

"Probably likes to hobnob with his fellow upper crust, I'll bet," Laszlo continued to ponder. "Mingle with movers and shakers in the Commonwealth, show off his money, that sort of thing."

"So if we could find someone special enough - a big enough deal - we could get them in as an inside man, have them pump him for information," Isis suggested.

"It'd have to be someone pretty special. Some fine, upstanding member of society, a leading light in the Commonwealth."

"Any ideas as to who that might be?" Captain Humboldt asked.

Everyone looked thoughtfully at him, and he looked back.

"... what?"

"You're a pretty special person, Captain," Isis said, looking Humboldt up and down. "I'm sure Sarm would be delighted to meet you."

"I'm not special!" Humboldt replied, almost defensively. "I'm just some Naval officer from the outskirts of the Commonwealth, why would Sarm care about someone like me?"

"Don't sell yourself short, Captain!" Laszlo chided. "You're the youngest captain in the First Fleet, and a gold pin graduate of the Academy... and let's not forget that little business with the Arrivene. Face it Captain, you're a superstar!"

"He has a point, Captain," the agent agreed. "No matter how you might downplay it, you have distinguished yourself quite a bit over the course of your career. And Sarm does like to meet such singular individuals."

Humboldt shuffled uncomfortably. "... fine. I can see I'm outnumbered here. Alright, so let's say I do get invited to his estate. What then?"

"Well, if I were some moneyed-up Central Province bigwig, I'd probably like to flaunt my collection of expensive things," Laszlo speculated, "conspicuous consumption and all that. He may well have some of it on display for visitors - maybe even the artifact itself. Take an interest - even if you can't see his security set-up firsthand, you may be able to get him chatting about it."

"You're sure of this?"

Isis shrugged. "We've stolen from enough people like him to know the type."

"Hmm, fair enough. And what will be your part of the plan?"

"We'll hang out somewhere in orbit," Laszlo answered, "there's bound to be an unregarded spot somewhere - an industrial module in the Ouroboros, maybe. Anyway, once you've got some idea of the artifact's security, send us a message on a coded frequency. We'll take it from there."

"Very well. Well, if we all know our parts, I suppose there's nothing more to decide," Humboldt said by way of conclusion. "We'll arrive in the Sol system in about twenty minutes, so I'll let security know to release all your equipment. Make whatever preparations you need to."

"Right you are, Captain!" Laszlo gave a playful salute as he and Isis filed out of the briefing room. As the door sealed behind them, Captain Humboldt let out a sigh. After a moment he raised a finger to his earpiece and called up the frequency of his chief security officer.

"Mrs. Almarn, this is Captain Humboldt. I'm allowing Mr. Hadron and Ms. Lagato access to the Wyvern. Have their gear returned to the ship, and ensure the ship is unlocked and ready for launch."

"Are you sure, sir? This is rather unorthodox." Captain Humboldt could almost hear the security chief frown disapprovingly over the comm.

"I'm sure, Lieutenant. Our current mission requires it."

"As you wish, sir. I'll see that it's done." Elindra Almarn was about as by-the-book an officer as they came, and all this underhanded need-to-know business was an affront to her sensibilities, though he knew she'd not even think of disobeying an order.

"Thank you, Mrs. Almarn. I realise this must be frustrating, but I appreciate your dutifulness."

"All part of the job, sir. Security out."

The link closed, and Captain Humboldt turned to the agent.

"Everything's in order, agent. We should have no trouble once we arrive at Sol."

The agent nodded approvingly. "Very good, Captain. And before you go, I'd like to echo your gratitude. This must all be a difficult pill to swallow, even without you and Hadron's personal history, but you've performed your duties admirably."

"Thank you, agent. It's just as Lieutenant Almarn just said, really: all part of the job."

Chapter 6

The invitation had arrived as soon as the Durendal had. The ship had only just emerged in normal space on the edges of Europa's gravity well, just over a quarter-hour after the briefing, and the email had arrived within seconds. Whether his arrival had been strategically leaked or if he just had his own connections, Captain Humboldt thought to himself, Sarm certainly wrote fast.

Once he'd ordered Sandersby to take the ship into dock, Humboldt approved the message and opened it. It was effusively complimentary, almost grovellingly gushing, and Sarm had taken great pains to express just how profoundly honoured his humble self would be if the noble and excellent Captain Elgar Humboldt would attend a pleasant social gathering that he was holding.

Elgar didn't know whether he wanted to laugh out loud or puke. Even ignoring the overly enthusiastic nature of the message, he just didn't relish the thought of spending an evening socialising with Central Province "elite". For all the Commonwealth had done to close the societal gulf between the old Empire's core and outer regions, there was still a lingering class divide that mere economic restructuring couldn't easily heal, and Elgar was proudly on the outer side. An old-money type like Sarm would ordinarily have barely paid someone like him any mind at all. But Sarm was careful to maintain a good public image, and that meant playing nice with the new order of things. Besides, as Laszlo had reminded him, Elgar was the fabled hero of the Battle of the Arrivene, and exactly the kind of figure that Sarm would be eager to be associated with. He'd done his best to avoid public attention, but Elgar couldn't completely outrun his reputation.

Elgar noticed that his finger had been hovering subconsciously over the delete button. He drew the digit back and gazed idly out of the bridge's dome. Europa was coming into view, with its lined surface that had always seemed to Elgar as though the creator of the Universe had left it in their pocket with their keys. As the Durendal began its final approach to the moon's orbital spacedocks, Elgar turned his attention back to the message. As much as he wanted to turn it down, he reminded himself that it was his duty to the Commonwealth to graciously accept it. Fighting the urge to sarcastically imitate Sarm's distinctive writing style, he sent back a reply confirming his grateful attendance.

"Docking complete, Captain. Powering down the engines," announced Sandersby.

"Your orders, sir?" Leurak asked.

"I imagine further orders will be forthcoming in due course, but probably not for a few hours," Captain Humboldt answered. "Inform the crew that they may consider themselves on shore leave for the next couple of duty shifts."

"Very good, sir."

"As for me, I'll be on Earth - duty calls. Have the captain's shuttle prepared for me."

"Aye-aye, sir. Have a good time."

Captain Humboldt gave a sardonic grimace as he stood up, before exiting the bridge. He made his way through the Durendal's upper decks, heading for the upper hangar bay.

The captain's shuttle had its own berth in the middle of the hangar's top deck, taking pride of place. Broad and low, hull designed with sweeping smooth curves, it was built primarily for luxury and status, quite in contrast with its functional and uncomplicated military surroundings. It was especially a stark contrast to the Department of Operations ship landed beside it, which seemed to have been carefully engineered to be as unremarkable as possible. It maintained the theme of nondescriptness that the Department preferred, also expressed as it was in its personnel, just like Agent CE362 who was standing patiently by its loading ramp.

"Good afternoon, Captain," the agent said as Elgar approached them. "Has Sarm contacted you?"

"He has," Elgar confirmed. "The email arrived right after the Durendal completed its jump. The man works fast."

"A good thing in this case, I think. All things considered, I'd rather not be left in suspense. Are Mr. Hadron and Ms. Lagato prepared?"

"I've ordered all their gear returned to them, so I imagine they've managed to get everything in order by now. I'll contact them when I set off."

"Very good, captain. I too have made the necessary arrangements for them."

Elgar cocked an eyebrow suspiciously. "Well, good. Might I ask what arrangements those might be?"

"You needn't concern yourself with them, Captain," the agent answered smoothly. "They will be taken care of when the time comes."

Something about this statement left Elgar feeling vaguely uncomfortable, but he shook it off. He saluted the agent and boarded his shuttle. Stepping into the cockpit, the consoles and panels came to life around him, as the ship recognised his rank and authority. As the low rumble of the reactor filled the ship, Elgar settled into the pilot's seat. He glanced over the start-up diagnostic as it came up full green, before reaching for the comm panel and dialling in the Wyvern's frequency.

*   *   *

Even after changing into her own clothes, which were rather more comfortable for her than the prisoner jumpsuit, Isis hadn't fully relaxed yet. The Durendal's security personnel had returned all of her and Laszlo's stuff to them, but she didn't trust them not to have attached some manner of bug or tracker to it. She'd spent the last twenty minutes investigating all the various nooks and crannies of the Wyvern for foreign devices. She hadn't found anything, but she wasn't planning to let her guard down. She was at least satisfied that there was nothing hidden in the living spaces of the ship. A more exhaustive search would have to wait until they were off the Durendal and she had the leisure to start taking off hull panels.

As she settled herself comfortably in the copilot's seat, watching out of the corner of one eye as diagnostic programs combed through the ship's systems, Laszlo stepped into the cockpit, wearing his characteristic spacesuit again.

"Aah, that's so much better!" he enthused, shifting its armour panels into place as he strode over to the pilot station. He dropped heavily into it, doing a full turn on its swivel in the process. "Did they take good care of the Wyvern?"

"Everything seems the same as before," Isis answered. "I didn't find any tracking devices yet - once we're landed in Earth orbit, I'll start checking the more secure compartments."

"Terrific. Any sign of Mat, by the way? I haven't seen them since we got EMP'd."

"Nothing in person, so to speak, but they left this in the computer for us." Isis handed a data tablet over the central console to Laszlo, with a message already on its screen:

"Las and Isis,
By the time you read this, I will have taken my leave of you. I hope you'll excuse the suddenness of my departure, but I'd rather duck out before Strannik or the Commonwealth get involved - I fear my presence would only further complicate an already "interesting" situation. Rest assured that I shall still be looking out for you and keeping an eye on the proceedings as they unfold. Good luck!
 - Mat"

"Well, that explains that, I guess," Laszlo said to himself as he finished reading. "You'd think their remote drone would have left some sign of an exit, though."

"Wouldn't put it past them to have figured out teleportation or something," Isis mused in response. "So, provisional pardon, huh?"

"Yes indeed. I almost didn't think they'd go for it."

"Does this mean we'll be going straight from now on?"

Laszlo shrugged. "Maybe... if I can resist the temptation. That said, it would mean giving up the Wyvern, and I LIKE this ship..."

At that moment, the comm panel chimed as a call came in. Isis brought it up, and the face of Captain Humboldt appeared on each of their screens.

"Laszlo, Isis." Although he'd moved past the point of sneering at the sight of them, he was still brusque. "Are you ready to commence the mission?"

"I've checked the ship over, and I think everything's good," Isis replied. "We're ready to go at your command, Captain."

"Fine. I'm heading to Earth now, so you'd best follow me soon after. Just to remind you, the pardon doesn't take effect until you've delivered the artifact into our hands. If you're detected before that, the Commonwealth will disavow any responsibility and you'll be on your own."

"We know, Captain. As long as your crew didn't fiddle with the cloaking device, that shouldn't be an issue," Laszlo said.

"I can assure you that we made no such changes to those systems," Elgar answered with a touch of indignation. "In any case, if you have things in order, then I'll let you proceed as you will. I'll be in touch in due course - Captain Humboldt out." He terminated the link and the screens went blank.

"Looks like we've been given our marching orders," Laszlo remarked.

"Looks like it. Shall we set off, then?"

Laszlo turned to his own comm panel. "Wyvern to hangar control, requesting launch clearance."

"Clearance is granted, Wyvern. You may launch when ready. Good luck out there."

As the hangar door lowered out against the Durendal's hull, the Wyvern was wreathed in the characteristic haze of light of its cloaking device. Invisible and undetectable, it lifted itself off its landing gear and drifted out of the bay on manoeuvring thrusters.

"So, what's the plan?" asked Laszlo, as he pulled the ship away from the Europa docking complex and into open space.

"Head for Earth," Isis answered after a second's deliberation. "There's bound to be some abandoned industrial space on the Ouroboros we can hide in. We'll wait there for Captain Humboldt to get back to us there. In the meantime, we can think things over."

Laszlo nodded and began priming the FTL drive for the jump. Glancing out at the Durendal, the little glimmer of the captain's shuttle was visible departing its upper hangar. Curving away from the destroyer, it pointed itself in the direction of Earth and, followed by the Wyvern, made the jump to lightspeed.

*   *   *

The view of interplanetary FTL from the captain's shuttle wasn't quite as abstract as metaspace, but it was still pretty weird. Objects moving past lightspeed interacted strangely with electromagnetic radiation, catching up with and overtaking photons. Light seemed brighter even through the polarised windows, and was tinged with blue and purple. A brief flash of complete blackness might have been the ship passing through Mars, protected by its nullspace manifold - a little trick Humanity had learned from the Suura a few centuries ago.

As the distance to Earth dwindled ever more and more, Elgar began the deceleration procedure. The ship's speed dropped sharply, and Elgar kept an eye on both numbers. With care, a competent pilot could drop out of FTL over a planet with just the right vector and velocity to enter a stable orbit. It was a simple enough trick for a person with a good head for numbers and a steady hand at the controls, and one just as easily left to the autopilot, but satisfying to pull off manually nonetheless. He stared intently at the readouts and poised his finger over the control panel as numbers scrolled past. At just the right moment, Elgar tapped a button. There was a flash of energy, like a bubble popping, as the manifold dissolved and the shuttle snapped back into non-zero dimensions. Its orbital trajectory quickly resolved itself - a perfect insertion! Elgar grinned to himself as he called up the comm.

"Welcome to Earth," spoke the automated voice of Earth Traffic Control after a brief moment, "please submit your name, registry, and intended destination.

"Captain Elgar Humboldt, shuttle registry SNTr-723-SOC, requesting permission to land in Terratropolis."

"Thank you. Your request is being processed. Please stand by."

As the voice of traffic control was replaced with quiet, generic music, Elgar took a moment to turn his shuttle and face the planet below. Where bright white clouds didn't hover over them, blue oceans glinted in the light of the Sun, girded here and there by landmasses coloured with green fields, yellow deserts, and silvery-grey cities. Arcing above it all, parallel to the shadow of the nightside, the metallic ribbon of the Ouroboros gently rotated, encircling the globe. It was only the second time in his life that Elgar had ever been to Earth, but in some way the sight of the blue marble still resonated deep within him as home.

"Captain Humboldt, your landing permission has been granted," Traffic Control said after a moment's planet-watching, "please begin descent procedures along the indicated vector. We once again welcome you to Earth, and we hope you enjoy your visit."

As the channel closed, Elgar took up the ship's controls again. He pointed the shuttle along the vector that had been transmitted to his computer, and gently took it down out of the crowd of vessels still waiting. Firmly in the grasp of the planet's gravity well, a few seconds' thrust was all that was needed to set the shuttle falling gently into the atmosphere.

Elgar turned the shuttle to face into its trajectory, then leant back in his seat. At this point gravity and momentum would do the piloting for him, and needed no more input from him until the shuttle would enter the atmosphere. With nothing needing his attention, his thoughts and his gaze strayed idly. He looked out at space and wondered for a moment if he might have been looking directly at the cloaked Wyvern.

He wasn't, of course - there was plenty of empty space around even as busy a planet as Earth, and Isis wasn't about to fly close to civilian traffic if she could help it - but Elgar's shuttle showed up clearly on its sensors. Neither Laszlo nor Isis paid the ship's signature any mind though, as they were more concerned with keeping an eye out for police vessels.

"Looks like no-one's seen us," Laszlo surmised, not looking away from his sensor display.

"You sure we can trust Captain Humboldt?" asked Isis. "I mean, there's nothing to stop him from tipping off the police about us."

"Oh, we can definitely trust Elgar - he's not exactly my biggest fan, but I know he's not the backstabbing type. It's the rest of the Commonwealth I'm not so sure about, especially with that agent from the Department taking such an interest."

"Mmm. Well, if something is up, then it seems they're not quite ready to spring the trap." Isis looked over her own sensors, looking for a good place on the Ouroboros to land. She soon found one and took the Wyvern down.

The Ouroboros loomed large before them on their approach, a staggeringly huge curve of metal that stretched for thousands of kilometres in either direction to vanish behind the shape of the Earth itself. Parts of the station were older than even the Solar Empire, and it had grown over the centuries as Humanity had explored and colonised more and more of the surrounding stars, expanding and incorporating smaller stations into its structure in much the same way. Miles upon miles of shipyards, factories, and habitats had multiplied to support an ever greater empire, until the station had become a complete circle just as its new namesake held its own tail in its mouth. It was a vital part of both the Empire and the Commonwealth's industrial backbone and quite possibly the largest single artificial object in the known Galaxy - only the Tygoethans' rumoured "warmoons" rivalled it in sheer scale, and few people seriously believed those could even exist.

Landing in the shadows by the base of a vast docking pylon, the Wyvern settled into its familiar state of patient lurking, silent save for short-range signals it used to tell nearby sensors what it wanted them to see.

"Stealth protocols all up and running," Isis said, poring over the ship's reports, "cloaking devices operating at full. No response from local traffic... we're good."

Laszlo nodded his acknowledgment and shut down the ship's engines with a little flourish. "And now, it's up to Elgar to do his part. Nothing for us to do but wait."

Chapter 7

Sitting in the middle of the Atlantic Ocean, midway along a superhighway stretching between Africa and the Caribbean, Terratropolis was the capital city of Earth, and thus also of two successive interstellar nations. It had long been the political and economic centre of the planet, and even before assuming this mantle it had been the planet's premier scientific institute. It was an artificial island rooted on the ocean floor, and both above and below the water the city was a crowded sprawl of urban and industrial development, glittering with city lights and bustling with vehicles moving to and fro. Above the ocean's surface the city opened up almost like a flower, its petals wide panels linked by encircling rings that acted as the ground on which honeycombs of streets were built, broken up at regular intervals by plazas and parks. Leading to the main body of the city from the south, wrapping over the highway, was Atlantic Spaceport. It was the city's main facility for orbital craft both civilian and industrial, and such starships as were equipped to deal with planetary landings. Captain Humboldt's shuttle was among this category. It glid in a shallow arc down towards the city, its manta-like shape a mirror to the creatures Elgar fancied might be swimming in the ocean beneath. The shuttle flew to a graceful halt over the broad flat roof of the spaceport concourse, hovering neatly within the pattern of lights marking out its landing space. The shuttle touched gently down, and fuel pipes and maintenance cables extended from the landing platform to connect to its various intakes.

Elgar stepped down the entry ramp, a suitcase in his hand, and walked off the landing pad. As his shuttle was lowered into the garage beneath the spaceport's deck, he turned to regard Terratropolis itself. It was his first time seeing the city in person. He made his way to the edge of the deck and leant on the railing there, and took in the vista in quiet contemplation. The sea breeze scent of the Atlantic filled his nostrils as he regarded the four centuries-old city, and Elgar felt a curious connection to his surroundings. It was a feeling that spacers sometimes felt upon visiting their species' home planet, regardless of what species they may be - a feeling that, despite having been born and raised hundreds or even thousands of light-years away, they had come home.

After allowing himself a few minutes' wistfulness, Elgar checked the time and soon took his suitcase down with him to the taxi rank below. Sarm's gathering wasn't starting until the evening, and he was a few hours early. Plenty of time to take in some of what the city had to offer - he was sure that the Navy would allow him a little shore leave. Even if he wasn't enthusiastic about his plans for the evening, he could still manage to have a good time before then.

*   *   *

Naval dress uniform was not designed with subtlety as a priority. Whereas the standard uniform was a tasteful pattern of navy blue and forest green, the dress uniform went straight for bright white with gleaming silvery inlay. Even the simple steel epaulette on the left shoulder which bore the wearer's name, rank, and assignment was overdone on this outfit - someone had seen fit to replace it with a gaudy, over-filigreed pauldron, that was lined with a gold-plated chain held in place by a clasp bearing the Naval insignia picked out with gleaming synthetic diamonds. Whoever had designed this outfit clearly had a rather romantic idea of what military personnel should wear, and a rather hazy idea of what comfort was. At that moment in time, Elgar would have given his left leg to get back into his service gear.

Then again, perhaps it was the company that Elgar was chafing at. The "upper crust" of the Central Province were no longer the hidebound aristocracy they had been in centuries past, ever since the efforts of the Commonwealth to even society out, but old habits die hard and their ethos of nobility was particularly resilient. No matter how much economic control was wrested from the core worlds, the scions of the old "noble" families still acted as though they owned the place, as though all their wealth and power was owed to them. For someone like Elgar, born and raised on an outskirts backwater, it was all he could do not to scream in their faces. He'd managed the best he could, consoling himself by mingling with the guests whose company he took to better than the others, thanks to their being more socially conscious and down-to-earth (ironically because they usually spent time away from Earth) and by enjoying the free drinks that were being served, whose company he took to quite well indeed.

He also did his best to play the part of someone with a deep interest in astroarchaeology, which was not a difficult role to play. Laszlo had pegged Areton Sarm as the type to show off his wealth, and his guess was right on the proverbial money - all around the ballroom were glass cases, each one containing an article of Sarm's collection of artifacts. They had come from every civilisation in this quadrant of the galaxy and from every period of history - from ancient Zilzari clay figurines, to early industrial-era Parahvian island maps, to hull fragments of famous Tygoethan warships from the Imperial Wars... all this and more besides was arrayed before Sarm's guests, like a private museum of Sarm's indulgence.

Elgar was studying one of the cases, containing instrument panels from a pre-nuclear Syohar lunar rocket, when he felt a smart tap on his shoulder and heard a petulant voice with a very refined accent.

"I say, dear fellow, could I trouble you for more drinks?"

Replacing his hat, Elgar straightened up and turned slowly to the owner of the voice, a short man in an expensive robe and what he assumed was the latest fashion in facial hair - either that or he'd had a terrible argument with a razor.

"I beg your pardon, sir?" he replied with an imperious glare, speaking in the icy, level voice he reserved for mouthy subordinates who didn't know when to stop digging themselves into a hole.

The man's peeved expression vanished as he saw Captain Humboldt in all his Naval finery, and his eyes flickered nervously around his steely gaze. "Oh, I say, I'm dreadfully sorry! From behind, y'see, I thought you were one of the help."

Elgar put on a disarming smile and dismissed the mistake with a wave of his hand. "Oh, no harm done. Blame whoever designed these uniforms, eh?"

The guest tittered politely, and partly out of relief. "Oh, I don't know. Rather more elegant than that dull old outfit you're stuck in on duty, no?" He ploughed on, ignorant of the brittleness about Humboldt's smile. "Anyway, how are you finding this little event, Captain?"

"It's... certainly quite something, that's for sure," Elgar answered diplomatically.

"Oh, quite so, quite so! Anyone who's someone finds their way here," the guest continued. "On that note, if you don't mind my asking, who might you be?"

"Me? Well, did you ever hear about the Battle of the Arrivene?"

"Arrivene? Arrivene..." The man's face lit up as he recalled the name. "Ahh! So you're that dynamic young officer who single-handedly fought off an entire Tygoethan invasion force!"

"Well, I wouldn't say single-handedly," Elgar said, valiantly trying to turn embarrassment into false modesty, "but yep, that was me."

The guest enthusiastically seized Elgar's hand and shook it as though he wanted to break it off and take it home. "I say, jolly good stuff, that! Jolly good!" Still gripping Elgar's hand, he leaned in for a conspiratorial whisper. "You know, I've never liked those Tygoethans. They're cold-blooded, you know, and they don't think quite like us..."

"Now now, Markahl, let's not bring politics into our little soiree, eh?" The new voice broke into the scene and cut Markahl off mid-rant, quickly followed by its owner - a portly gentleman of an almost regal bearing, wearing a tastefully opulent robe and carrying a champagne flute. He laid a hand companionably, if pointedly, on Markahl's shoulder. "We've just put out a few bottles of Chateau Lumiere - 2565, a very good vintage - and I do know that's your favourite, yes? You simply must have a glass, old boy."

Whether he'd taken the hint or just wanted a drink, Markahl nonetheless pried himself off Elgar with one last shake of his hand. Elgar's rescuer turned back to him with an apologetic grimace.

"I daresay all this upper-class snobbery must be a bit much for a child of the colonies such as yourself, Captain?"

"It's not my usual wheelhouse, I must admit," Elgar answered, vaguely wondering if he'd just been inadvertently insulted. He dismissed it and extended his hand. "You'd be Areton Sarm, I presume?"

"The very same, Captain. It's a pleasure to finally meet you." Sarm's genteel handshake was a bit of a relief after Markahl's overeager wrenching. "I'm simply honoured that you accepted my invitation."

"As am I to have received it, sir. You've put on quite a fine party."

"Oh, too kind, far too kind!" Sarm gestured towards a quieter corner of the ballroom, and Elgar followed. "As I said, I'm glad you came to my little gathering. I feel that it's important for my class of people to maintain ties to the wider Commonwealth, you know."

"We're all better off together, that much is certain," Elgar politely agreed.

"Very much so. If nothing else, we can avert unfortunate happenstances like the Interregnum. Grim business, that."

Elgar nodded. "Oh yes. My homeworld was ruled by the General until I was five. Wasn't much fun for us, I'm sure you can imagine."

"My word!"

"Mmm. Luckily, we were liberated by the Commonwealth. That really changed everything for us - it brought new life to the planet, new opportunities."

"And that's really it, isn't it?" Sarm concurred. "Opportunity! As fond as I am of my peers in the Province," he said, gesturing broadly towards the rest of his guests, "they mostly just grouse about how the Commonwealth is changing the ways we used to enjoy - taxes and the like, the usual story. But you and I, Captain? We've seized the chances that the march of history presents us!"

Elgar deftly snatched a glass from a passing waiter's tray and raised it in toast. "I'll drink to that!" The two of them clinked glasses and swigged heartily from them. As he lowered his own, Elgar looked around the room with an appreciative eye. "And it's obvious how well you've seized the opportunities of this brave new world."

Sarm smiled smugly to himself, reminding Elgar of a gilded toad. "I have managed to do fairly well for myself, it's true." If he was trying to feign modesty, he wasn't very good at it.

Elgar swallowed his proletariat indignation and soldiered on. "Well, it's not many people who could come to own Humanity's largest private astroarchaeological collection."

Sarm's face lit up at the mention of one of his favourite subjects. "Ah, you have an interest in astroarchaeology, Captain?"

"Oh yes! It's a fascinating field, and you're quite a big name in it." This wasn't quite true - Elgar ordinarily had merely a polite appreciation for it, but no real investment. Nonetheless, he'd done a bit of research to maintain the illusion. "I understand at one point that you even possessed one of the Voyager probes?"

"Indeed I did, Captain! Voyager 1 itself... a beautiful piece, you know. It really was one of the crown jewels of my collection."

"What happened to it?"

"The Commonwealth Academic Institute did." Sarm's enthusiasm and reverence for the topic faded, and was replaced with venom. "After all the work I'd done getting the thing, and they suddenly decided that they wanted it for themselves. Kept badgering me with ever-increasing sums, and insisting that it was "part of Humanity's historical legacy". The gall!"

"You didn't agree with them?"

Sarm seemed to become conscious of what he'd said, and picked his next words carefully. "Well, you mustn't misunderstand me, Captain. History is certainly an important part of our culture, and I suppose really such things must belong not to one person, but to all Humanity." It was a carefully constructed speech, and it seemed clear that Sarm didn't really believe it. "Anyway, I eventually caved and sold Voyager off. Made quite a nice little profit, if I may say so - afforded me quite a few choice pieces... but it wasn't really the same, you know."

"So no plans to sell any more of your collection?" Elgar sipped his drink with nonchalance, trying to look as innocent and devoid of ulterior motive as he possibly could.

Sarm smirked and playfully waggled a beringed finger at him. "Now, now, Captain! If I didn't know any better, I'd say you were trying to weasel another of my crown jewels out of me!" He glanced conspiratorially around and leaned in a little closer, speaking a slightly hushed tone. "The Academic Institute have been trying to get their hands on another of my artifacts lately. And you know, if anything they've been even more eager about this one."

Elgar leaned in too. "What artifact might that be?"

"A relic of the Sagittarian Empire. Here, I'll show you..." He led Elgar over to one of the display cases. It contained a golden replica of the early Suura exploration vessel Grylan, but as Sarm called up a control panel and pressed a few buttons the model starship flickered and vanished, quickly replaced with a hologram of another relic. Elgar recognised it immediately - it was unmistakably the third Sagittarian shard.

"If truth be told, I've no idea what this actually is," Sarm began, gazing at the shard with an admiring eye, "but I have a strange feeling that it may be perhaps the most important relic I've ever owned. I'm told that it dates back to the same time as the Sagittarian Extinction, two million years ago. That means that whatever its true meaning, this curious objet d'art might well be the last work of art ever created by the Sagittarians. Can you imagine it, Captain? The last glimmering of an ancient species' twilight, in my possession. It staggers one to think about it..."

"It certainly does," Elgar agreed, studying the shard closely. "I think I can see why you'd be so loath to sell it off."

"Oh, indeed. After the wrench of selling the Voyager probe, I don't intend to let any more of my favourites go, no matter how much anyone offers." Sarm's voice had turned hard, and his expression jealously possessive. "I'll protect it with my life."

"Speaking of protection, I notice that this is a hologram," Elgar said, waving a hand in the shard's direction. "That's a pretty clever trick, I must say. Are all the cases just projectors?"

"Oh, yes! I'm no fool, Captain. All my artifacts are stored in a secure vault - I purchased some space in the old Arcology and had it closed off for my own private use. The only access to my storehouse is an elevator in my study. I'll happily show off my collection to my friends, but the artifacts themselves?" Sarm gazed at the shard's hologram avariciously. "They're just for me."

Sarm returned to the moment and looked back at Elgar. "Anyway Captain, it's been simply marvellous chatting with you!" He seized Elgar's hand again and shook it heartily. "But now I must attend to my other guests. Please, enjoy your time in my humble home."

With that, Sarm bid Elgar goodbye and vanished into the crowd of other guests. Finally free of Sarm's company, Elgar let out a long sigh of relief and drained the rest of his drink in one long swig. He left the glass on top of the display case and made his way out of the ballroom and onto the balcony. Night was falling over the Atlantic, and the Sun was dipping below the horizon. In the evening sky above, the lights of the Ouroboros could be seen curving over the Earth, perpendicular to the axis of Sun and Earth.

Elgar gazed out at the scene for a moment, watching the comings and goings of skycars, smelling the scent of salt on the breeze. Eventually, having unwound just a little, he pulled a datapanel out of his pocket, entered a frequency, and began typing.

"Have concluded recon on Sarm. Intel follows..."

Chapter 8

"Shard found. Located in secure vault in Arcology - ocean floor. Access via elevator in Sarm's study. Getting late, party winding down - recommend getting underway within next few hours, before dawn. Good luck."

Isis was lying on her bed as she read Captain Humboldt's missive, having just enjoyed a few hours' peaceful sleep after a comprehensive bug sweep of the Wyvern, inside and out. It was useful in busy situations like this that her bio-engineered physiology could get all the rest it needed from brief, irregular periods of sleep, although if anyone called it a "catnap" to her face she'd kick them in the shins.

Setting her datapanel to one side, she sat up on the edge of the bed, pulled on her boots, and made her way to the Wyvern's cockpit. She glanced briefly at local sensors, but it seemed no-one had found the ship. Satisfied that they remained undetected, she called up meteorological reports and began plotting a flight plan.

It was several minutes later that the cockpit door opened again, this time to admit Laszlo. Unmodified as his genome was, he was rather slower than her to properly wake up, and was making do with culinary assistance in the form of a mug of coffee. He shuffled his way to Isis's station and set a second mug on a safe space on her console.

"Morning..." he mumbled in bleary greeting.

"You mean evening," Isis replied, not looking up from her screens. "At least it is over the mid-Atlantic."

"Ugh, wha'ever. Doesn't mean anything in space anyway."

Isis picked up her mug and took a sip of coffee. It was a blend common among people who lived and worked in space, having originated with the Solar Navy Starfigher Corps where it had picked up the name "fighter fuel". Perfect for people who might need to be up and about at a moment's notice, it was generally agreed to have roughly the same awakening powers as a red alert, but much less likely to disturb one's bunkmate. Still, even to those who had acquired a taste for its thick, bitter flavour, it was a hell of a thing to subject oneself to first thing in the morning, and Isis couldn't help the fur on her cheeks bristling and her whiskers twitching. Laszlo was much less prepared for it, and his face was curled up in an involuntary grimace.

"Gyurgh..." he opined once he had control of his facial muscles again. He gave his head a hard shake and went back for another swig now that he knew what he was up against. "So, evening over the Atlantic? Does that mean Elgar's come through for us?"

"It sure does. Latest message in the comm log is from him."

Laszlo called it up and gave it a read. "Hmm... should be doable, wouldn't you say? No word about what security to expect, though."

"I don't suppose Sarm was giving tours of his private vaults. But hell, we made it through Sel'Akis - what more could this guy throw at us?"

Laszlo grinned in agreement. "So, what's the plan?"

"I'll take the Wyvern down to Terratropolis slowly - don't want to make a fuss of atmo entry if we can avoid it. Shouldn't be more than an hour. In the meantime, we'll get suited up and ready... unless you really want to tackle this one in your dressing gown?"

"Don't think I couldn't pull that off," boasted Laszlo, getting up to leave, "but I might as well do this by the numbers. A little too much riding on all this, eh?"

As the pair began their preparations, the Wyvern unclasped itself from the inner surface of the Ouroboros. For a few moments it simply drifted away from the station, before reorienting itself onto an entry vector and setting off on the path down.

*   *   *

Elgar Humboldt had never in recent memory felt quite so relieved as he had upon leaving Areton Sarm's party. He'd made his excuses and left shortly after his talk with Sarm - claiming to be on "important Naval business" wasn't a complete lie, in his defense, but it was certainly more polite than the more accurate reason of preserving his sanity. So eager had he been to get back to familiar ground that he didn't even stop to have a rest in the hotel room he'd rented for his brief stay on Earth - he'd changed into civilian clothes, gathered up what little luggage he had, and set off for the spaceport with barely a pause for breath. By the time Sarm's party was drawing to a close, the captain's shuttle was already in orbit and priming for the journey back to the Durendal.

Elgar didn't feel the need to manually pilot the shuttle through FTL this time. He set the autopilot and stepped out of the cockpit into the cabin. In the few minutes while the ship flew back to Europa, Elgar changed once again into his service uniform. Examining himself in the mirror, satisfied that everything was on straight, he replaced his hat with a flourish. Although his dress uniform was no less official than this one, for the first time today he felt properly dressed - he felt like Captain Humboldt again.

Reentering the cockpit and resuming his seat, the Captain checked the ship's position and saw that the shuttle had almost arrived at Europa. He glanced up out of the window just in time to see the nullspace manifold dissolve. The Jovian moon and its orbital facilities were arrayed before him.

An automated voice chimed in. "This is Europa Naval Facilities Control, please state your identity and destination, and await confirmation and approval."

"ENFC, this is Captain Elgar Humboldt. Requesting permission to land on the SNV Durendal."

"Vocal patterns confirmed. Welcome, Captain Humboldt. Now transferring you to SNV Durendal - please stand by."

"Got you on sensors, Captain. Enjoy the party?" The image of Oleg Volkash, scarred and weathered from a lifetime behind starships' guns, appeared above the shuttle's main console.

"Don't ask, Mr. Volkash," Elgar answered, smiling back at the first familiar face he'd seen all day. "How's the Durendal?"

"Still just as you left her, Captain. The technicians give her a clean bill of health."

"Glad to hear it. Permission to come aboard?"

"Granted, Captain. Welcome home."

The comm line closed, and Elgar took the shuttle back to its berth aboard the Durendal. As he stepped down the entry ramp he fell naturally into the confident, determined stride of a starship's commanding officer. He made his way in this gait to the bridge where Volkash was waiting for him.

Volkash tore off a salute. "Captain on the bridge!"

Elgar returned the salute. "At ease, Commander."

"And how was Earth, sir?" asked Volkash, idly glancing through ship diagnostics on the main holoprojector.

"Oh, let me tell you, it was just the most fun I've ever had!" Captain Humboldt's voice was heavy with sarcasm, before he let out a groan of sheer exasperation. "Stars above, Oleg, if it weren't for the free bar, I could've screamed."

"Sounds like a fine old time, Captain!"

Humboldt rolled his eyes, before he shook the frustration off. "How about you, Commander? Get up to anything on shore leave?"

Volkash shook his head. "I've barely left the Durendal, really. Had a few drinks with the rest of the senior staff, but nothing other than that."

"Really? No desire to see the sights of Sol? No family to pay a visit to?"

"Not with a few thousand light-years - all my relatives live in the Bastion Province. And I'm not much for tourist things. Staying on the ship is fine by me." Volkash shrugged. "I've gotten into the habit. Married to the job, you might say."

"I suppose after almost forty years of service, you might well be," Elgar said thoughtfully. "Ever considered applying for your own command? You certainly have the experience."

Volkash looked pensive for a moment. "Sometimes I think about it - and the Navy has offered it once or twice..." He shook his head. "But no, Captain, I've never really wanted the big chair. I've found my niche, and the Navy appreciates that. I like to think I'm pretty good at being a weapons officer."

"Well, you'll do until someone younger and prettier comes along," smirked Elgar.

"Oh, Captain, you wound me!"

At that moment, a trilling chime alerted Elgar to a new call - one marked for his attention only.

"If you'll excuse me, Mr. Volkash..." He stood up and moved into his office to take the communique in privacy. As he sat down, the monitor in his desk flashed into life. He called the communique up, and the face of Agent CE362 appeared before him.

"Welcome back, Captain. How did you enjoy Areton Sarm's party?"

"Don't ask," Elgar muttered sourly. "Anyway, to what do I owe the pleasure?"

"New developments, and subsequently new orders. We've successfully located Morgan Strannik's ship - it's currently in FTL transit in the Inner Province. A Naval battlegroup is moving to intercept."

"Well, excellent. And our orders?"

"The Durendal is to join this battlegroup and lend assistance. Once the Corsair is neutralised, you are to secure the artifacts in Strannik's possession, pending further instruction."

Captain Humboldt's brow furrowed. "Surely the battlegroup is more than up to the challenge presented by one pirate vessel? One extra destroyer isn't going to be much in the way of reinforcement."

"It's not a question of reinforcement, so much as it is one of discretion. The fewer people who are aware of the Sagittarian situation, the better. Vice Admiral Elrey has granted the Department his permission to deploy you as necessary, so you needn't be concerned on that score."

"If you say so, Agent," said Elgar skeptically. "And what about Hadron and Lagato?"

"The Department has that matter in hand as well. Don't worry about it."

Elgar cocked an eyebrow, and paused for just a moment before speaking again. "I suppose I'll have to take your word for it, Agent."

"Rest assured Captain, this is a very important matter, and the contribution of you and your crew is invaluable. Department of Operations out."

The Agent's image cut out, leaving Elgar alone. He stared at his reflection in the blank screen, deep in thought, before calling up another frequency. After a moment or two, another face appeared on the screen - worn by age and experience, and dressed in much the same uniform as Elgar himself.

"Good evening, Captain," said Vice Admiral Elrey, a familiar smile on his face. "How's the Durendal holding up?"

"Glad to say she's in tip-top shape, Admiral. I hope I'm not interrupting you?"

"Not at all, Captain. Things are nice and quiet here. What can I do for you?"

"It's about our assignment to the Department of Operations, sir. I just wanted to confirm that you've given your permission."

Elrey's smile curled into a faint grimace of disgust. "Ah. That." He cleared his throat and settled himself. "I can tell you that all the necessary procedures have been taken, and it's been properly cleared with the Admiralty. Administratively, it's all perfectly above aboard."

"Has the Department told you anything about what's happening?"

Elrey shook his head sourly. "Nothing whatsoever, Captain. All I know is, you came to a Department ship's rescue and now I've had one of my destroyers co-opted for some damn cloak-and-dagger business."

"I don't like this any more than you do, sir," Elgar replied. "I'll be glad to get back to the battlegroup where I belong."

"You and me both, Captain. The sooner this can all be done with, the better. For now, just get this done with as best you can, and hopefully you can come back into the fold soon."

"I'm looking forward to it, sir. But I have my orders, and we need to get underway ASAP."

"Very well, Captain. Make us proud. SNV Trajan out."

The two officers exchanged salutes and Elrey closed the channel. Elgar was, if not fully mollified, at least soothed by his superior's shared dissatisfaction with the whole affair. Still, he did indeed have his orders and he had to follow them. He rose to his feet and stepped back out onto the bridge.

Volkash was leaning over the navigation console as Elgar entered. "Captain, the ship received a set of coordinates from the Department of Operations while you were taking your call. Do we have business in the Inner Province?"

"We do, Commander. Our mission takes us to a battlegroup intercepting a pirate cruiser."

A trace of confusion crossed Volkash's weathered face. "And our... business on Earth, sir?"

"Apparently, that will be taken care of in our absence." The Captain shrugged and shook his head. "Don't ask me, I don't really understand any of this myself."

"May I speak candidly, Captain?"

"Of course you may, Commander. What's on your mind?"

"This mission from the Department - I don't like it one bit. In fact, none of the crew are happy about this. They're still behind you as they should be, but... we're being used, sir. Everyone's thinking it."

"You're preaching to the choir, Oleg. I don't like this any more than they do." Elgar let out a long, weary sigh. "I trust everyone can still be relied upon to do their jobs?"

"Oh, no question about that, sir. No matter what, they're still your crew."

"Glad to hear it. Hopefully we won't need to put up with all this much longer. For now though, I'll have to call them back from shore leave. We've got work to do."

*   *   *

Eyes in the dark looked in, and watched the situation unfold. Possibilities were calculated. A message was sent.

"We need to talk. Things are reaching a critical point."

"What's the problem?"

"Our mutual friends are in danger."

"Is the situation compromised?"

"No. The threat is from within."

"The Department?"

"Yes. They intend to arrest them."

"Damn. They never tell me anything upfront."

"Our friends' good will towards you is crucial. If things are to proceed amicably, intercession will be required."

"I can't act openly. What would you suggest?"

"A neutral third party. Someone with no formal link to the Commonwealth, or to our friends."

"I think I know someone suitable. I can explain a few things to her, and she'll help."

"She can be trusted?"

"I'd trust her with my life."

"Excellent. She only needs to warn them - they are resourceful enough to escape. I'll provide precise details now"

"Data received. I'll contact our third party now and get her up to speed. Keep an eye out."

"Of course."

One message ended, and another began.

"Hello, Artemis. I hope you're well. I have a favour to ask of you."

"It's good to hear from you, Alex. I'm in good shape, thanks. What can I do for you?"

"I have some friends who will shortly need help out of a sticky situation."

"What exactly is the situation?"

"The short version is, they're on Earth and need help evading the police."

"Earth? This wouldn't happen to be something to do with the Sagittarians, would it?"

"... how much do you know?"

"I know about the Extinction, and I know a bit about the artifacts. And I know you wouldn't get personally involved unless it was important to the Commonwealth."

"This must remain secret. You mustn't breathe a word of this to anyone, understood?"

"Breathing's never been an issue for me. But I do understand. Don't worry, Alex, I can be discreet."

"Thank you. And our friends?"

"I'll keep an eye out, and do what I can for them."

"I appreciate it. Remember: discreet."

"Understood - don't worry, I know a few tricks. Artemis out."

*   *   *

With a clear and cloudless night having drawn in, there wasn't much to distinguish the view of the Atlantic from that of orbital space above. Between black sky and black sea, only the city lights of Terratropolis could be clearly discerned, and it was towards these that the Wyvern was flying. Coasting silent and invisible over the water's surface, well below the level of air traffic, it drew smoothly up to the city. Sarm's estate sat on its own section of groundplate suspended away from the main body of the city, mounted on the plateau top of a spire rooted in the ocean floor. The mansion and its grounds sat peacefully in the dark of night, unaware of the starship looming silently above.

Her hands at the ship's controls, Isis studied the sensor readouts and examined the layout of the mansion. Whatever kind of security Sarm may have had in place to avoid prying eyes like this, the Wyvern's military-grade EMDAR sneered at such civilian measures, no matter how expensive they were.

"Sarm's vault is supposed to be on the ocean floor," Laszlo said as he studied the readouts himself, "so I'm guessing we just need to find the top of that reinforced shaft." He waved a finger over his screen at the shaft in question, which ran the full height of the estate and straight down into the spire on which it rested. It stood out clearly on the screen like the proverbial sore thumb - whereas the mansion's architecture was built for the sake of opulence, the elevator owed its design to the pressures of the deep Atlantic.

"And it looks like the entrance is in his study," Isis continued, "which opens onto a nice open balcony. How considerate of him to leave us enough room for the loading ramp."

"What kind of defenses are we looking at?"

"Pretty comprehensive camera coverage, security sensors... and a meteor-proof shield over the whole estate." Isis barely looked away from her piloting as she set anti-security systems in motion. "Nothing we haven't seen before. Not even worth worrying about, really."

"I suppose Sarm wasn't expecting an attack from thieves with military-spec gear, huh?" Laszlo said with a grin.

Isis smirked back, before making the last few adjustments to the ship's course. "I'll set the Wyvern hovering over the balcony. We'll have to mind the step coming down - and those planters - but we should be able to leave her there while we get the shard. There's so much EM activity from the city that any of our emissions will be covered up nicely."

"And we can handle any security from then on?" Laszlo asked.

"Easily, I'd say," Isis answered with confidence, as she set the controls and stood up from the console.

The two pirates descended through their ship to the cargo bay. Isis shut the lights off, before lowering the cargo ramp. The pair stepped down and hopped down onto Sarm's balcony. As they passed through the Wyvern's double-layered shield, the noise of the ship's engines suddenly went silent. If anyone had been watching the pair, it would have seemed as though they'd simply appeared from thin air and stepped down onto the balcony.

Isis strode up to the study's wide doors, quickly picked the lock, and held the door open for Laszlo. If Sarm did have a lot of work to do in his day-to-day life, it looked like he didn't do much of it here. A pentagonal room with three glass walls looking out on the ocean view, the study was sparsely furnished to keep it bright and airy. In the room's centre was a broad office desk, on which there was little in the way of paperwork or stationery. Against one of the back walls was a cosy reading nook by a wall full of bookshelves, which Sarm apparently got much more use out of - the cushions of the seat were sunken in from frequent sitting, and a small pile of well-worn novels sat under the reading lamp - and set into the other back wall were the double doors into the master bedroom, slightly ajar. Laszlo sidled carefully up to them and peered in - Sarm was fast asleep, the very picture of peaceful slumber. Laszlo gingerly closed the doors and locked them.

"Sweet dreams, you rich git," he whispered, before turning back into the study. He cocked an eyebrow at Isis, who nodded back. She turned back to studying the room intently to find the entrance to the vault elevator. She raised a finger to point it out: a seemingly innocuous bookshelf.

Laszlo's eyes widened in excitement. "He hasn't... tell me he has!"

Isis stepped up to the bookshelf, giving it an appraising look as she squinted one eye oddly to dial another setting into her retinal implants. She raised one hand and hovered a finger over the spines of some of the books. Eventually she stopped at one of the tomes, whose binding was just a little off-colour, and which the implant indicated had electrical leads connected to it. She rested her fingers upon it as if to pull it from the shelf, but the book only tilted out on a hinge. There was a soft "click", and the entire bookshelf swung silently into the wall, revealing a short passageway leading to a sturdy metal door.

Delight bloomed on Laszlo's face at the sight, and he bounced gleefully on the balls of his feet. "Oh my gooood, he has one of those!" he enthused, barely managing to keep his voice to a hoarse whisper. "I've always wanted one!"

Isis rolled her eyes. "Calm down, Las. Anyway, you live on a starship - where would you put it?"

Laszlo pouted in a feigned huff. "Oh fine, spoilsport, ruin all my fun."

The metal door slid aside, and the pair stepped into the elevator therein. Laszlo pressed the down button, and the lift began its abyssal descent. In accordance with inexorable ancient tradition, Laszlo and Isis both fell silent and stared straight ahead. Everything was quiet save for the soft whirr of the elevator's machinery...

Br-r-r-reep!

The unexpected "incoming comm" tone from Laszlo's wrist computer almost made the two of them jump out of their skins, but he raised his arm and popped up the panel. The contact frequency wasn't one he recognised. He glared suspiciously at the holopanel as he ran programs to counteract any tracking attempts, before finally accepting the call.

"Who is this?" he demanded by way of greeting.

"A friend of a friend, Mr. Hadron," came the reply. The voice was strong yet sonorous, every word seeming perfectly enunciated.

"Whose friend?"

"You don't know them personally, but they're well connected and have your best interests in mind."

"How do I know I can trust you, or this friend?"

"I promise you that I'm on the level, but I concede you have no reason to believe me. You can heed or ignore what I want to say as you please."

Laszlo cocked a querying eyebrow at Isis, who shrugged back.

"... alright, "friend", we'll hear you out," Laszlo decided. "What did you want to say?"

"I need to warn you: the Department is setting you up."

"What?!"

"The police are waiting for you in orbit - they've been tipped off. The moment you leave the atmosphere, they'll pounce on you."

"I knew it," muttered Isis.

"What about our rendezvous?" Laszlo asked, concerned and confused.

"It seems it's been cancelled. The Durendal has been ordered to help apprehend Morgan Strannik in the Inner Province. They undocked a few minutes ago. By the time you have what you came to get, they'll be light-years away."

"Well, what are we supposed to do now?!"

"Get arrested, I suppose, and have the artifact confiscated from you, if the Department has their way."

"Gee, thanks."

"All's not lost. I have the coordinates for the Durendal's destination, and I'd be happy to pass them along for you."

"And what do you get out of this?"

"I'm not doing this for my sake. Call it a friendly favour, if you like."

Laszlo muted the channel and lowered his wrist, brows furrowed in thought. He looked at Isis. "Think we should trust this person?"

"Hrrmmm... well, either we're being set up for a trap in orbit, or in the middle of nowhere in the Inner Province." She shrugged. "Or maybe both. But I like my chances a lot better out there than I do over the capital of the Commonwealth."

"I guess at least in deep space we have the chance to check things out. More leisurely than here, anyway."

Isis nodded. "It'll be easier to run from a trap without Earth in the way, that's for sure."

Laszlo turned things over in his head for a second, then raised his wrist again and unmuted the call. "Alright, friend. Give us the coordinates."

"Certainly," the voice said, "sending them now."

The coordinates came through as promised, and Laszlo checked their position on the galactic map - they indicated an empty patch of space well off the usual beaten path, but both Laszlo and Isis recognised it as not too far to a remote underworld outpost.

At that point, the lift reached the bottom of the shaft and stopped. The doors slid open to reveal a pitch black room beyond.

"Well, this has been delightful," Laszlo said, stepping out into the darkness, "but we really should be going now. Thanks for the coordinates."

"You're welcome, Mr. Hadron," the stranger replied. "I'll keep an eye on things up here for you. Good luck."

The connection closed, and Laszlo shut his wrist panel. "Well, wasn't that pleasant?"

"Mmm. D'you think it was Captain Humboldt's idea or the Department's to bug out and leave us holding the bag here?" Isis asked wryly.

"I really hope it wasn't Elgar's idea. I don't think he'd actually suggest it himself, but... well, it has been a while." He shrugged, and looked around at the darkness surrounding the little island of light cast by the open elevator. "Dark in here, isn't it?"

"Let me just get that..." Isis said, stepping up to a console in front of them, its glowing display the room's only light. She studied its security for just a moment, before tapping one of the buttons. Above them, the room's lights gently came to life, igniting slowly to give their eyes time to adjust. Row after row of lights began glowing, systematically illuminating the room before them, revealing just how large it was. They could quite happily have landed four of the Wyvern on a floor this big, and eight more on top of those. At least, they could have done were it not for Sarm's collection. Rows of display cases were lined up in neat ranks up and down the lowest level, the aisles between them carpetted in plush red, each one containing a rare and valuable artifact. At regular intervals up the cliff-like steel walls were balconies ringing the vault's interior space, each one filled on all sides by even more artifacts. In the empty space between the balconies were suspended a few especially large pieces of Sarm's collection - a small herd of various extinct creatures, some taxidermied and some mounted skeletons, standing, swimming, and flying with a Tyrannosaurus rex bringing up the rear, under the carefully restored hulls of a wing of fighters that dated back to the Tygoethan Wars.

"Well..." Laszlo began, gawking in amazement, "isn't this a neat little collection?"

"Nothing little about it," Isis muttered in awe. "How much d'you think all this must have cost?"

Laszlo's mental calculator grappled with the question before quickly admitting defeat. "I dread to think." He turned his gaze to Isis, grinning like a loon. "You don't think maybe we've got time for a little shopping, do you?"

"Sorry Las, but we've got a job to do," Isis answered as she looked back at the console to call up a directory of the collection. "Looks like each of these display units has its own security node - I don't like the chances of trying to crack more than one of them without tripping the alarms. Besides, we're gonna have our hands full getting the artifact to the Wyvern. Anything more would just be a hassle."

"Aw, go on, please? How about the T. rex? Just its skull?"

"Now, now, Las, having a pet is a very big responsibility... here, I've found it." Isis peered over the railing and pointed to one of the cases on the lowest level. "Right over there. Follow me."

The two pirates made their way to an elevator in the corner of the room, which took them down to the bottom level. They followed one of the aisles, eyes lingering on many a spotlit display case. Even the artifacts they couldn't identify at a glance they could tell were each worth a small fortune - altogether, for the money that Sarm must have spent assembling this collection, he could probably have bought a small moon. It was all Laszlo could do not to drool. His fingers were twitching avariciously as he gazed at the treasures around them. "... maybe if we got a crew together... fly in on a hollowed-out antiproton hauler..."

Isis glanced back at Laszlo. "Did you say something?"

"Just thinking about how we could smuggle all this out of here. This could be the biggest score since..."

"I seem to recall you not being too happy about pulling off a job on Earth not long ago."

Laszlo shrugged. "Greed changes one's priorities, what can I say?"

"Keep your head in the game, Las. This would only be a big score IF the police don't come down on us first - and need I remind you, if our new friend is to be believed, they're lurking in orbit right now to do just that."

"Right. Yes. Sorry." Laszlo gave his surroundings one last lingering gaze, before refocusing his attention. "Eyes on the prize."

"Speaking of which..." Isis stopped in front of the display case she had been leading them to. Inside was the unmistakable shape of a Sagittarian shard, though the little plaque in the corner of the case just said "Unidentified Sagittarian artifact, circa 2 million years old".

"Jackpot."

Laszlo studied the shard, and its case. The display unit was plain and undecorated, designed not to draw attention from its contents or give any indication as to security measures. From a brief glance, though, Laszlo's practised eye could already see a few things: a fine mesh pattern in the glass indicated an optic web to detect breakage, and a flat bundle of wires led from one side of the case's surface to under the shard - pressure sensors, most likely. The spotlights were also suspicious, covering the shard even from angles that weren't readily visible to an onlooker - probably motion detectors. Last but not least, the faint seams of a panel could be seen in the top corner of the front of the case.

Isis was also examining the situation. Her ocular implants illuminated all the things Laszlo had noticed, and about a dozen more that were hidden from the unmodified eye. She double-checked her neural rig to ensure that the vault's digital security was sufficiently blind to them, before pulling her combat knife from its sheath in her boot and using it to pry the panel open. She dropped down on her haunches to examine the controls therein more closely - a number pad and a keyslot were the two most visible measures in place, but Isis's augmented senses also revealed biometric sensors in the pad's buttons. Simply knowing the code wouldn't have been enough to satisfy it, you'd need Sarm's fingers to enter them. Just under them, concealed under a little door of its own, was a small microphone.

Isis stared thoughtfully at all this for a quiet moment, before nodding to herself. "Easy."

Laszlo had expected nothing less from his partner in crime. "Excellent. If you've got this under control, then I'll just nip off and sort something out. Call me if you need a hand."

"Las, don't do anything stupid. We need to stay focused."

"Please, just trust me. I'm not planning to endanger the job."

Isis gave Laszlo a long stare, but eventually nodded in assent. "Okay. Do what you need to do." She pointed a thumb at the shard. "Just don't be too long, I'll need your help carrying this thing back to the Wyvern."

"Fret not, I'll be back in a few minutes." He turned to leave, then paused and turned back. "Just out of curiosity though, you wouldn't happen to know what the ocean pressure down here is, would you?"

"Um... what? I dunno... I guess we're about 3,600 metres down, so..." Isis shrugged, nonplussed. "Why do you need to know that?"

Laszlo didn't answer for a moment, rubbing his chin in thought. "Hmmm... never mind, I'll sure we'll be fine. I'll leave you to it for now. Back in a moment."

With that, Laszlo turned around again and set off at a brisk pace down the aisle. Isis watched his retreating form for a moment, her face a mask of bewilderment, before shrugging it off and turning her attention back to the display case. In the time she and Laszlo had been talking, her hacking suite had already divined all the input that the security panel was expecting. Some of the biometrics were harder to fool than others - she briefly toyed with the idea of heading back up the lift and cutting Sarm's finger off for the DNA, but charitably dismissed it as too cruel. The voice lock probably required an input other than him screaming in pain anyway. In any case, there were other ways past the system.

Though they were mostly covered in fur like the rest of her genetically altered body, Isis's fingers had areas of bare skin at their tips, much like the toes of an ordinary cat. By design her pads had no fingerprints, as they were an identifying mark that a career criminal like herself could do without. But with the help of a few black market nanotech mods, that merely left them a blank canvas. As she reached into a pocket for something to fool the keyslot, she loaded the fingerprint profile from her sensors into her index finger. It tingled itchily as the surface of her skin tinted itself with a mottled metallic grey and nanobotically reformed itself into the desired shape. She flexed her fingers to dismiss the pins-and-needles sensation as she held up what would take the place of the key. Like her fingerprint, it too was a work of nanotechnology, growing from stored polymers and alloys out of a coin-sized unit into a functional replica of the real key.

Isis would have to work quickly, as she reasoned that the systems were probably also on a timer to check for hesitancy that might indicate duress. She inserted and turned her fake key - the lights around the lock turned green in confirmation - then entered the code into the keypad with her altered finger. There was a pause of a few seconds as the system looked for a DNA pattern, while Isis's hacking software tried to fool it. Soon enough though, the keypad glowed green as well, and the door of the microphone snapped open. Isis's hand came out of her pocket again, this time holding something the size of a cigarette lighter. She held its end up to the microphone and pressed the device's button.

"Areton Sarm, code four-four-two-four-omicron-omega."

To any human listener, the imitated voice wouldn't have sounded quite right at all - the tone and cadence were both flat and unconvincing, more like a musical instrument that for some reason produced the sound of that phrase in that voice - but it was well within the parameters that the voice lock was programmed to accept. The door snapped shut again, and the panel flashed gently with a happy little beep of acceptance. A holographic control panel appeared in the air before it. Isis stood back up, returning her gadgets to their pockets. She shut down all the case's remaining security measures and opened the display case.

The glass panels slid down into the body of the case to leave the shard exposed. A faint but distinctive scent met Isis's nose, musty and reminiscent of petrichor. The ancient spaceport on Eurus had smelled much the same as this, as had the Euran shard itself. It was the unmistakable smell of two million years of history. This was definitely not a hologram or a replica.

Isis paused for a moment, simply staring at the ancient metal fragment before her. Astroarchaeology wasn't really her field, but she still couldn't help but feel a subtle sense of awe at the sheer scale of time it represented. After a second or two, she pulled herself back into the current moment. She bent down to grasp the shard and carefully lifted it off its stand. The shard was heavy enough that moving it any real distance was a two-person job, and Isis could only just get it clear of the case. Grunting with effort, she managed to lower it to the floor without dropping it. Standing up, she looked around for any sign of Laszlo, but he was nowhere to be seen.

Isis put a finger to her earpiece. "Las, where the hell are you?"

"Just sorting something out, Isis," Laszlo replied. "Be there in a minute!"

It was rather more than a minute before Laszlo finally came back up the aisle to find Isis sitting against a display case, playing a game on a handheld device to pass the time. At the sound of Laszlo's booted feet, she looked up from her screen to greet him, but she smelled him before she saw him.

"... why do you smell like seawater?"

Laszlo's armour was glistening with moisture, and his cloak was dripping on the carpet. "Like I said, I was sorting something out. Anyway, shall we get this thing out of here?"

Isis saved her game and put her console away, and shifted herself over to the shard. With Laszlo grabbing the other side, they managed to lift it up between them, and started down the aisle with it between them.

"What exactly were you "sorting out" that made you so wet?" Isis asked, giving Laszlo an odd look as he walked backwards ahead of her. "Because if you're proposing that we swim back to the Wyvern, I remind you that I haven't really dressed for abyssal weather."

"No no, nothing like that," Laszlo said dismissively. "But I was thinking of a way to evade the local police on our escape. D'you remember that time a couple of years ago when we avoided that mercenary gang by hiding in a gas giant?"

"Yeah, I remember that. So, you've brought the Wyvern down here to the bottom of the ocean?"

Laszlo grinned proudly. "There's an airlock at the end of this room - must be from way back in the day when it was still Arcology property. Managed to dock the Wyvern on the other end. Would you ever expect to find a starship on the sea floor?"

"I would not, I'll give you that." Isis frowned thoughtfully as she thought things through. "So that's phase one of the plan, but how are we actually going to get out of the system? You haven't actually answered the big problem."

Laszlo would have shrugged if he didn't have several kilograms of ancient metal weighing down his arms. "We can just make a metaspace jump once we've undocked."

"... are you sure that's safe?"

"No, but I never think too hard about safety - rarely have the time. How bad could it be?"

They continued into the airlock, the inner door of which Laszlo had left open. He hit the control panel, and the heavy door sealed behind them. Things were still and silent for a moment, as the aging computers calculated the necessary changes in pressure and atmosphere, before the outer door slid aside. Beyond was the tall triangular passage of the Wyvern's collapsible docking tube, its end wrapped airtight around the airlock's entrance and its floor glistening with puddles of salty water.

"I guess this thing's not built for deep ocean pressure, huh?" Isis noted as she sloshed into the tube.

"It's fine, just had a bit of trouble draining all the water out," Laszlo replied. "I'll check the fluid valves once we're underway."

The pair of pirates continued into the passage. Through the inflated nanopolymer walls of the tube, they could hear the low rumble of the Atlantic around them. The passage was only extended a few metres, but things were a little too close for Isis's preferences and she was quite relieved to emerge in the Wyvern's cargo bay.

As the door sealed behind them, Laszlo and Isis found an empty crate for the shard and lowered it carefully inside. Free of its weight, Laszlo stepped back over to the airlock and pressed the button to retract the tube. He turned back to Isis, beaming.

"Well, that went well, didn't it?"

"Don't pat yourself on the back just yet, Las," Isis answered as she sealed the crate. "We've still got to get out of this system, remember?"

"As I said earlier, no trouble at all. We have those coordinates, and all this seawater should easily mask our jump trace."

The pair made their way up to the cockpit. It was hardly unusual to see black through the windows of a starship, but it seemed to be a distinctly different texture of darkness to that of space - thick and oppressively close, rather than empty and distant.

"Handling's a bit odd down here..." Laszlo muttered idly to himself as he pulled the ship away from the vault. "Must be water currents pushing us around."

Isis stood just behind him, leaning on the centre console. "Are you absolutely sure this is going to work? Because I've certainly never heard of a sub-oceanic FTL jump..."

"It'll be fine, don't worry," Laszlo said soothingly. "How often do you hear about starships actually landing in deep water at all?"

"Well, never, but that's probably because it's not a good idea."

"It's not standard procedure, certainly, but... well, look, the Wyvern's a freighter, yes?"

Isis looked doubtful. "Yes, so... ?"

"So it's designed to fly with a wide range of mass, from cargo bays empty to stuffed to the rafters. Any seawater we take with us is just like that hypothetical cargo. It's just outside the ship rather than in it, that's all."

"I guess that makes sense, but how is all that loose water going to react when it's no longer pressed in by the rest of the ocean?"

"The Wyvern's strong enough to handle a change in pressure like that. It wouldn't be the worst thing she's had to deal with. After that, it's just ice buildup, no trouble at all." Laszlo turned his head to smile reassuringly at Isis. "I have thought all this through, I'm not a complete idiot."

Isis cocked an eyebrow and gave a little wry smirk. "Maybe not completely... but if you do break the ship, you're paying for it."

"Duly noted. Anyway, I've got our cause plotted. Buckle up..."

What happened next would become a little mystery to years to come - the "oceanic thunderclap" that had rung out in the mid-Atlantic with no explanation and seemingly no source, that would be occasionally be speculated about by those interested in the unexplained. But just for tonight it went all but unnoticed, save for seismological sensors and a lot of very confused fish - the Wyvern left Earth almost as unobtrusively as it had arrived.

Chapter 9

Beyond those within the Central Province, the Challenger Trail was one of the oldest trade routes in Human-controlled space. For most of its length it followed the flight path of the ship it was named after - the TEV Challenger was one of Earth's first faster-than-light exploration vessels, among a fleet of six ships designed and constructed in a hurry after the destructive Solar War to search the stars for new worlds to sustain humanity. The path taken by the Challenger had led it along a trail of promising systems, with planets both rich in resources and with environments amenable to human habitation. After the first wave of colony ships had laid the foundations of what would become the Central Province, the second wave had followed in the Challenger's footsteps to form the core of the Inner Province, and one of the main economic arteries of both the Commonwealth.

The first major port of call along the Trail in the Inner Province was the planet Khepri, and the area between its system and the border of the Central Province was designated the Delta Sector. A trade route this busy was a natural target for piracy, and it was the mission of battlegroup 4-Gamma-Sixteen to keep the people and cargo on the route safe. The general profile of this mission was mostly a preventative and reactive one - maintain a presence to discourage pirate attacks, and respond to the ones that did occur - and rarely involved more direct action than that. This was mostly due to the persistent evasiveness of local pirate operations. No amount of recon flights or surveillance probes had turned up any reliable intel on pirate bases in the area. But on rare occasions, the endless sifting through space would turn up something promising.

The SNV Khopesh lurked patiently in deep space far from any stars, surrounded by the battlegroup of destroyers and frigates that she was the flagship of. The massive Archipelago-class cruiser dwarfed all of them, like a shark in a school of piranhas. Among that shoal of lesser vessels was the Durendal. None of the battlegroup's crew were quite sure why the Durendal needed to be here. They had all already heard of Elgar Humboldt before this mission - in fact, just about everyone in the Solar Navy had. His exploits as a fresh-faced first officer in the Battle of the Arrivene almost three years ago were legendary: forced to assume command of both the damaged cruiser and its battlegroup when a rogue Tygoethan invasion force had ambushed them, he had managed to hold off the tactically superior force for over an hour before reinforcements could arrive to drive the armada off. Though he always maintained that luck played a greater part in the victory than his tactics or his courage, he had proven beyond the shadow of a doubt that he could get the job done. No-one doubted that for a moment, but they still questioned the necessity of having him assigned to this mission.

The briefing hadn't painted a terribly intimidating picture, after all. One pre-Interregnum heavy frigate with little hope of reinforcements, up against a Naval battlegroup... it was hardly the most imposing opposition. 4-Gamma-Sixteen was more than up to the task of handling the Corsair without the Durendal's backup. But Captain Humboldt had been quite clear that the Durendal's marines were to be the tip of the spear in the boarding action. They would be first in, and they would be moving to secure the cargo hold.

"What cargo are we fighting for?" Rear Admiral Selene, the Khopesh's commanding officer and 4-Gamma-Sixteen's leader, had asked.

"I'm afraid that's on a need-to-know basis," had been Humboldt's answer. And that had been all that was said on the matter. The Captain had apologised for the pervasive secrecy of the whole affair, but everyone still felt like they was being left in the dark. That agent from the Department of Operations quietly observing things from the sidelines didn't help matters much.

But whatever misgivings there may have been about the mission, they had a job to do. The ships of the battlegroup, and the Durendal, were all in position. All they were waiting for now was the Corsair...

*   *   *

Morgan Strannik was not by nature a trusting man. A lifetime of bitter experience had taught him that other people could be relied upon to get what they wanted out of you, then discard you once you were of no further use. Nonetheless, even with this informing his philosophy, he knew that some things needed outside expertise. Tracking down and securing the Sagittarian shards was turning out to be one of them. He wouldn't have admitted it aloud, but it was mostly thanks to luck that he had managed to acquire the first two - by the time his contacts had given him the locations of the shards, the one on Eurus was already gone. Laszlo Hadron was far from Strannik's favourite person in the Galaxy, but he had to concede that he and that cat woman worked fast. The EMP trick was a desperate gambit that he hadn't expected Hadron to fall for, but if Morgan had taken the time together a proper operation for Sel'Akis he would have missed his chance by days. Still, now that the Navy had got their hands on them, they wouldn't be a problem any more. He could organise the raid on that millionaire's stash at his leisure.

He leaned forward in his captain's chair. "How far out are we from the signal point?"

His first mate Ankerak's antennae twitched in attention as xe checked the data. The Ylerakk turned to face xir captain, revealing the thin strips of metal holding xir facial carapace together.

"Only a couple of minutes out, Cap'n. I'll get the broadcast code ready, shall I?"

"Yeah, you do that, Rak." His question answered, Strannik leaned back into his customary slouch and stared idly out into metaspace. The Station - no-one had ever really bothered giving it a name - had always been a secretive place, even in its early days during the Interregnum when it was a waypoint for smuggling expensive goods out of the Central Province's sealed borders. Its location was a carefully guarded secret, and liable to change without warning as the facility was towed around the cluster of stars it called home under a powerful cloaking device. Only with the correct codes would the Station contact you with docking instructions, and beyond that it was silent and unseen. The Commonwealth had long suspected the presence of the Station but decades of vigilance had turned up nothing, and after all this time they had more or less given up searching. There was no reason to expect anything except empty space.

"Dropping out of transit in three, two, one..."

Metaspace rolled back away from the Corsair, and normal space replaced it.

It was not empty.

"This is Rear Admiral Zarya Selene of the Commonwealth warship Khopesh, to the starship Corsair. You are wanted for numerous counts of piracy and smuggling, and are suspected of carrying stolen cargo. You are ordered to power down weapons and engines and prepare to receive boarders."

A cold chill ran collectively down the spines - and equivalent anatomy - of every person on the Corsair's bridge at the sight of the Commonwealth flotilla surrounding them. Horrified silence descended on the room, as Ankerak turned to Morgan.

"... Cap'n?"

Strannik was no less terrified than his crewmates, but as their leader it fell upon him to put on a brave face. He swallowed his fear, cracked his knuckles, and scowled at the Khopesh.

"Like hell we will! All power to weapons and shields, evasive manoeuvres!"

The bridge was a flurry of frantic activity as everyone leapt into action. As the Corsair began turning, Strannik called up his chief engineer on the comm.

"Vorruhl, get that drive charged up! We need to get out of here!"

"No good, Cap'n. They're generating an interdictor field - we can't initiate interpolation."

Strannik muttered a vicious curse as he closed the channel, turning his attention back to the bridge. "Then we'll fight our way out."

"Fight our way out?!" The weapons officer stared back at him in incredulous anger. "We're gonna fight our way out of a Navy battlegroup?!"

"That's what I ordered you to do, isn't it?! Now get to it!!"

Surrounded on all sides, the Corsair's shields flashed to full power, as its missile banks opened and its turrets swivelled into position, like a predator baring its teeth. The Navy response was immediate - as the venerable pirate vessel turned to present broadsides, the first few shots from the battlegroup struck home.

The Corsair fought with vicious desperation, and the Navy ships with practised precision. Harrier frigates bore down on the Corsair, their heavy guns pounding its shields relentlessly, as fighter-bombers wove deftly around volleys of searing energy to lend their own ordnance to the fray. Assault destroyers encircled the battle to fence the Corsair in, while their longer-ranged cousins moved into position to pin the pirate ship in a crossfire.

It was a rout, and everyone knew it. The Corsair was pathetically outmatched. As warning alarms signalled the imminent collapse of the shields, Ankerak turned away from xir console and looked up at Morgan on the high dais of xir captain's chair.

"Cap'n, we've lost this. We need to power down and rethink our strategy."

Morgan didn't spare Ankerak more than a distracted glance, fixated on the battle plans on the bridge screens. "We have not lost, Ankerak, and we're not going to--"

"DON'T BE A DAMN FOOL, MORGAN!!" Strannik fell silent, shocked back into the moment, and stared at his first mate. It was rare enough for Ankerak to raise xir voice to take notice when xe did.

"We are not going to win this one, not like this. You know what we have to do."

Strannik continued matching glares with Ankerak, until the shields finally failed. The unprotected ship lurched alarmingly as short after shot hit home.

The voice of Rear Admiral Selene cut in once more. "Starship Corsair, you can neither escape nor defeat us. I say again, power down your weapons and engines and surrender. Make this easy on yourselves."

In the flickering lighting of the bridge, Ankerak's gaze met Strannik's again. Strannik folded first.

"... seal the upper decks. Prepare for boarding plan six."

As his crew moved to carry out his orders, Strannik stewed in impotent fury. Sometimes he really hated it when Ankerak was right.

*   *   *

Agent CE362 was taking some time away from their assignment, though not by their own choice. They had requested to remain on the Durendal's bridge before the battle had begun, to properly observe that things went smoothly, but Captain Humboldt had insisted that Naval protocol demanded the confinement of all non-essential personnel to quarters in a combat situation. What the agent knew of the battle plan didn't lead them to think that the Durendal was in any danger, but they knew better than to press the issue -

although they still weren't terribly happy about being deemed "non-essential".

They were occupying the time by catching up on their paperwork. The Department of Operations' own protocol required that missions be documented in their entirety, to ensure that all activities had an eye kept on them - that the watchmen were watched, as Department operatives often said about it. The agent typed away at their personal terminal (Department agents didn't use non-Department systems if they could possibly avoid it, as they could all too easily be compromised), faithfully recording all of the events of the mission, but every few minutes they switched windows to check on their messages. There was an air about them as they carried on with their work: not quite of impatience, but certainly rather pointedly expectant. They were waiting for something, and it was taking its sweet time.

"This is Commander Leurak to all Durendal crew. Combat situation has been resolved, alert status is now green. You may resume general stations."

The agent looked up at the announcement, and noticed that the orange lights that had been gently pulsing for the last half-an-hour or so had finally switched off. The agent activate their comm.

"Captain Humboldt? Come in please."

"Captain Humboldt here. What can I do for you, Agent?"

"I take it from the Commander's announcement that the situation has calmed down somewhat?"

"That's correct, Agent. Morgan Strannik has been dealt with. You can leave your quarters now."

"Excellent, Captain. May I return to the bridge now?"

"Very well, if you feel it necessary. Come on back up."

"Thank you, Captain. I shall see you shortly, then."

With that, the agent saved their report and made a brisk pace back up to the bridge. As they stepped into the room, a few of the officers there glanced up from their consoles, only to snap their attention back. Agents from the Department often had that effect on a room.

It fell to Captain Humboldt to be a little more welcoming, though there was still a touch of reluctance about his attitude. "Agent, welcome back! We were just finishing up here."

"So I see, Captain. What's the status of the Corsair?"

"Disabled, and currently being towed into the Khopesh's hangar bay. Our marines are on-site to board and secure the shards."

The agent nodded approvingly. "Well done, Captain. A very efficiently conducted operation."

"I think the Khopesh and her battlegroup deserve the credit for that, but I'm sure they'll appreciate it. What about the third shard, on Earth?"

"No need for you to be concerned, Captain," the agent replied smoothly, "that situation is under control."

"Well, that's good," Captain Humboldt answered with just a little edge to his words, "because as far as I can tell, things are going to be a bit up in the air."

"As I said, Captain," the agent said, fixing a steady gaze on the Captain, "the situation is under control. You don't need to worry about it."

The two stared at each other for a brief but tense moment. "If you say so, Agent," Humboldt finally said, not breaking his stare.

"I do say so. In fact, I'm expecting an update any moment now-_"

"Captain, there's a ship dropping out of metaspace."

Captain Humboldt tore his attention away from the agent in an instant. "Who is it, Sandersby?"

"They're not transmitting any recognition codes. Scanning now... looks like a civilian freighter, heavily modified. Also detecting... salt water?"

Captain Humboldt blinked. "Salt water?"

Sandersby shrugged. "That's what the sensors tell me, Captain - traces of salt water covering the hull."

A trill came from Torzay's console on the other side of the room. "They're hailing us, sir, "she reported, "shall I put it through?"

"Yes, Ms. Torzay, thank you." Captain Humboldt straightened his uniform. "Maybe they can explain it."

A hologram of the freighter's pilot resolved before him. "Hello, Captain! It's just us."

"Laszlo?! What are you doing here?"

"I could ask you much the same question - we thought you'd be sticking around in Sol so we could make this delivery. Er, by the way, those Navy ships are getting a bit close. Could you... ?"

"Of course. Ms. Torzay, put me through to the battlegroup." Torzay called up the frequency, and nodded to the Captain.

"Battlegroup 4-Gamma-Sixteen, the recently arrived ship and its cargo are expected. Do not engage."

"Looks like they're backing off," Laszlo noted, "thanks for that. So, what does bring you out here, anyway?"

"If you must know, Mr. Hadron, we were assisting in the apprehension and capture of the Corsair and its cargo. Your arrival is rather timely, if unexpected."

"Well, well, well! Nicely done, Captain!" There was more than a little smug satisfaction in Laszlo's voice. "I suppose that means once Isis and I have handed off our trinket, you'll have the complete set? Speaking of which, d'you want it now?"

"Yes, no time like the present. I'll contact the cruiser Khopesh and secure landing permission for you. Wait for further instructions. Durendal out."

In the cockpit of the Wyvern, Laszlo leant back in the copilot's seat. A broad smile had spread across his face.

Isis glanced over at him. "Someone's having a good day, eh?"

"Morgan Strannik in Commonwealth custody... never thought I'd see the day! Would it be petty to call him up just to gloat, d'you suppose?"

"Yes, Las, incredibly petty."

"Eh, probably. Can we at least get a look at the Corsair?"

Isis shrugged and turned back to her controls. She checked the sensors to pick out the Corsair, then turned the Wyvern to face it. The battle had left it in a sorry state, with its hull ruptured in several places and a few of its weapons missing altogether. With its engines disabled, it was under the power of tugs from the Khopesh - a horde of little craft clinging gravitically to its hull, moving the stricken frigate around with surprising ease, dragging it into the Khopesh's cavernous main hangar.

"Aaah, that's the most wonderful thing I've seen all week." Laszlo put his hands behind his head and admired the sight with a smirk of near-infinite smugness. "Delicious schadenfreude!"

At that moment, the comm chimed. Laszlo sat back up as Isis accepted the call. "Starship Wyvern, this is the SNV Khopesh. Captain Humboldt of the Durendal has requested that you be granted landing permission to transfer sensitive cargo. Once the Corsair is secured, we'll transmit an approach vector."

"Acknowledged, Khopesh. Standing by."

"Looks like that's our marching orders sorted out," Laszlo observed. "And I suppose we'll have to turn over the Wyvern too." He let out a long sigh, as his mood sank at the thought.

"There'll be other ships, Las," Isis said, though it was clear that the platitude wasn't much comfort to her either. "But I'll miss her too."

Laszlo nodded distractedly, then stood up. "Well, I might as well start packing up our things. Who knows, maybe we'll get lucky and something'll come up..."

*   *   *

The Khopesh's main hangar was divided into two flight decks surrounding a large central space. Because gravity in interplanetary space is largely a question of personal choice, the decks were both oriented vertically relative to the rest of the ship, facing inward towards each other. Standing on one deck and looking up, the other deck would hang above like a ceiling, ships and personnel hanging from it like roosting bats. At this moment though, part of that view would have been blocked by the Corsair. It was secured in extendable gantries like a helpless rodent clutched in a bird-of-prey's claws. On the nearest deck, squads of marines waited as engineers worked on breaching the hull. With this mission before them, no-one really paid much attention as the Wyvern landed several metres away.

The Wyvern was not unattended, however. In the landing zone next to it sat the Durendal's captain's shuttle, and standing before it was Captain Humboldt and another squad of marines. They watched the Wyvern as it landed and its engines shut off, not looking away for a moment even as it sat still on the deck. Eventually the cargo ramp extended and Laszlo stepped out to meet them.

He moved slowly as he made his way down the ramp, wary of the steady gaze of the Navy marines upon him - not to mention Elgar's - and swallowed nervously. For a tense second, neither he nor the Naval personnel made a move. Eventually Laszlo started walking towards them, trying to look as unthreatening as possible, resisting the urge to put his hands over his head.

"Captain Humboldt. Always a pleasure."

Elgar nodded curtly back. "Laszlo. Is the item ready for transport?"

"Mm-hmm. Crated up in the cargo bay. Go ahead and take it."

"And Ms. Lagato?"

"She's packing up our stuff. Once we've got it all out, she'll hand over the keys."

"Very good. Thank you." Elgar waved a hand in the direction of the Wyvern, and the marines marched towards it, leaving him and Laszlo alone on the deck.

An awkward silence settled over them, disturbed only by the industrial susurrus of the hangar. Eventually Laszlo cleared his throat and broke the silence.

"So, what's to become of Isis and I?"

"Once we've secured your shard and you've surrendered the Wyvern to us, your conditional pardon guarantees your freedom," Elgar answered. After a brief pause, he snapped his fingers, remembering something. "And the Eaglehawk too. You'll have to hand that over as well."

Laszlo pouted. "Bugger. I was hoping you'd forgotten about that."

"Nice try." Elgar flashed a wry smirk, and looked up at the Wyvern thoughtfully. "Truth be told, I almost didn't think we'd be meeting like this. I half-expected that you'd try to run or something, if you'll pardon my saying so."

Laszlo shrugged, unoffended. "I won't say the thought didn't cross our minds. But trying to go to ground in the Central Province would have been tricky, to say the least. Plus, we've never had a full pardon on the cards before. It's an interesting opportunity."

The two men turned to look out at the stars. "What are you planning to do with your new-found freedom?" Elgar asked, not entirely unsuspiciously.

"I dunno, really. We could do anything we wanted, I suppose. Who knows, I might even go straight."

"Now that would be a surprise!" They both shared a quiet chuckle.

The two fell silent once more, and once more Laszlo spoke up. "What about you and me, I wonder? Things can't go back to the way they were before, but..."

Elgar sighed ruefully. "I don't know, Laszlo. It's been a long time, and some wounds are hard to heal. I can't imagine your convictions have changed..."

"No. They haven't." Laszlo was quiet but firm on this point.

"I thought not." Elgar looked away. "Neither have mine, come to that." He returned his gaze to Laszlo, with a hopeful smile. "Still, you've proved that a lot can change. Maybe--"

"Captain."

The two looked back in the Wyvern's direction. The marines were exiting the ship, with the shard's crate between them.

"Preliminary scans indicate that the artifact is genuine."

"Excellent, sergeant. Pass it over to the inspection team and let them have a look at it."

The marine sergeant saluted, and gestured to her men to hand the crate over to some technicians standing nearby. They immediately began looking it over with their instruments.

Laszlo gave Elgar a weary look. "Really, Captain? Is your trust still so thin?"

Elgar looked back with just a touch of sheepishness. "Just due diligence, Laszlo. Besides, would you be completely trusting in my position?"

Laszlo shrugged, conceding the point. "I suppose not." He looked away from the crate, idly staring into space, until his gaze found the Corsair. "Bit of a sorry sight, isn't it?"

"Hmm?" Elgar looked up at the disabled frigate as well. "Oh. Yes, the Navy don't faff around when it comes to fighting."

"Clearly not. Did you remember to disable the emergency power loop?"

Elgar furrowed his brow. "The emergency power loop? But that's just for life support, surely?"

"Oh, it's an old Privateer trick - if you hook the reactor ignition system into the emergency power loop, you can start the ship back up after it's been disabled. It puts a lot of strain on the systems, but if you don't mind that then you can get your ship back up to fighting trim in an emergency."

Elgar's expression turned to horror at this revelation. Realising the implication, Laszlo's face fell too, and as one the two men turned to look at the Corsair again.

As if cued by the mere action, the frigate gave a sudden roar. The engines flared and guttered, sending tremors through the gantries restraining it. The Khopesh's personnel scattered in alarm, and the Corsair's gun turrets began to move...

Elgar didn't remember much of what happened next. Alarms started blaring just before the Corsair began shooting, and everything turned to pandemonium. The pirate vessel seemed to be primarily aiming for the boarding teams, but in practice it was a free-for-all - virtually anything it could hit was a worthwhile target. The captain's shuttle erupted into a gout of flame, throwing everyone nearby to the floor under a hail of debris.

Laszlo had a little more presence of mind in this chaotic situation. He scrambled to his feet and tried to survey the scene. Past the blinding, scorching wreck of the shuttle, he could discern armoured figures striding across what was left of the flight deck. They walked with purpose among the carnage, and the rain of fire from the Corsair turned aside before their approach. They weren't Navy.

Dragging Elgar onto his feet and after him, Laszlo started back towards the Wyvern. The Naval marines and technicians were already fleeing into it as the pirates fired on them, moving to surround and secure the shard's crate. Laszlo shot back at them but he knew it was no contest. He concentrated on herding the stunned Elgar up the Wyvern's cargo ramp. As the Captain scrambled dazedly up the ramp, Laszlo backed into the bay and sealed the door behind him.

Isis stood amidst the survivors, rifle in hand. "Las, what the hell is going on out there?!".

"The Corsair," Laszlo answered, turning to his partner and holstering his gun, "it wasn't as disabled as it looked."

"And the shard?"

"Gone. Strannik had boarding teams of his own ready."

"Well, shit. What now?"

At that moment, Laszlo felt an armoured hand land on his shoulder and spin him around.

It was the marine sergeant, her expression all business. "The Solar Navy is hereby commandeering this vessel, civilian. We'll take it from here."

Laszlo bridled at the order and shoved the sergeant's arm away. "Like hell you are! Sit down and shut up, Navy, or I'll boot your arse out and you can try your luck back on the Khopesh."

"This is an emergency situation, pirate," the sergeant spat back, bringing her hand to her sidearm and her face close to his, "and threatening a Navy marine is a very serious offence!"

"I don't threaten, I promise! Isis-- !"

"Under Commonwealth authority, you are ordered to-- !"

"Commonwealth authority can go f-- !"

"BOTH OF YOU, SHUT UP!!"

There was no arguing with that tone of voice. Both Laszlo and the sergeant fell silent, staring at surprise at Captain Humboldt.

"Sergeant, stand down. One pirate shootout is quite enough for one day!" The sergeant let go of her gun and stepped back with a salute.

"Laszlo... thank you for taking us aboard." Elgar gestured to the marines and technicians who had survived the Khopesh's hangar. "But we need to return to the Durendal right now."

"... fine. You're welcome, by the way. Isis?"

"I don't know, Captain. With the Corsair back in the fight, it's going to be difficult to land on your ship."

"I'll see what I can do." Elgar brought a finger to his earpiece. "Captain Humboldt to Durendal, are you reading me?"

"Affirmative, Captain. What's going on over here?"

"I'm on board the Wyvern with Laszlo Hadron. The shard is in Morgan Strannik's hands. Stand down from combat and we'll dock to--
"

"Negative, Captain Humboldt." It was Agent CE362. "We don't have time to transfer personnel. Under emergency directive 14, I'm hereby assuming temporary command of the Durendal until the Corsair and the shards are both safely apprehended."

"Agent, the Corsair is surrounded by a Naval battlegroup! Even without the Khopesh, it isn't going anywhere."

"That may not be true, Captain," interjected Sandersby. "The Corsair's charging its stardrive. They're getting ready to jump."

"Mr. Volkash, can we disable the Corsair before that happens?"

"Negative, Captain. They're using the Khopesh's hangar as cover. We might destroy the Khopesh if we fire on the Corsair."

A sudden tremor rumbled its way through the ship.

"Captain, they've made the jump."

"Sandersby, trace its trajectory and plot course to match!"

"No need, Captain," Isis spoke up. "Tell them to set course for Eurus."

"Eurus? What do you... ?"

"Strannik has the shards, but he doesn't know what to do with them," Isis explained, "so he needs to find someone who does. Best guess, that someone is on Eurus. Put out an emergency call and you can intercept him before it's too late."

"... of course! Humboldt to Durendal, set course for planet Eurus, maximum speed!"

Chapter 10

The Corsair always ran a bit rough, being as old and weathered as it was. As with any complex machine, in operation its various systems made a lot of subtle sounds and vibrations that someone familiar with it could pick up on and thus gauge its condition. The emanations currently coming from the Corsair were not good sounds - all that business with the Navy battlegroup had taken its toll on the vessel, and it was being pushed close to its breaking point. Morgan Strannik was not a terribly easygoing man at the best of times, but with the strained symphony of his ship's struggling systems ringing in his ears, he was especially on edge.

Still, part of him felt in subconscious response to this, it wasn't all bad. The Corsair wasn't flying smoothly, but it was still flying. That meant a lot to a Privateer, especially to one who had just been disabled and almost captured by a Commonwealth cruiser. No matter how bad it gets, common Privateer wisdom held, as long as you can still get yourself moving, you're still in the game.

Ankerak entered the bridge and walked up to Strannik's chair, diagnostic report in hand. "The Corsair's running as well as can be expected, Cap'n. The cold start did a number on a lot of systems and we're barely up to basic operating condition, but repair crews have the worst of the damage locked down. We can keep going for now."

"Good. Are we still on course for Eurus?"

"Looks like it," the navigator answered, "the stardrive held out better than other systems, so it should be fine." Ankerak paused to clear xir throat pointedly. "Cap'n, are you sure this is the right course of action? Wouldn't it be smarter to go to ground and wait for the heat to die down?"

Morgan shook his head. "Not likely. The Commonwealth would never admit it, but this shit's big. They're not going to let this go as long as those shards are in the wild." He turned his head to arch an eyebrow at his first mate. "And with that kind of heat, d'you think the underworld is gonna let us stay hidden?"

Ankerak turned away, antennae twitching. Xe didn't speak for a moment. "What does all this even lead to, Cap'n? What the hell even is the Wargod's Tomb?"

"The riches of a dead empire? A really big gun?" Morgan shrugged. "Whatever it is, we don't have much choice but to see this through. I guess we'll find out along the way."

Ankerak still seemed doubtful, but presently shrugged them off. "So what's the plan?" xe asked.

"Get the crew together - those that aren't holding the ship together. I think it's time we did something with the rest of those EMP mines."

*   *   *

Lorentz Kellermann's life had been quite a long one so far, and much of it had been defined by Eurus and its ruins. Unlocking the Sagittarians' secrets had been his focus and his fascination for as long as he had been studying astroarchaeology, and he had dedicated his career to it. He had sometimes been asked whether this single-minded pursuit had caused him to miss out on a lot of what life had to offer, but he never really felt that way. Living a conventional life was all well and good for those interested in doing so, but it wasn't for him. To help focus the lens of history was a rare skill, and to have shed light on a mysterious civilisation by his studies was as fulfilling a legacy as he could hope for.

With the storm season in full swing, there was no real work to be done on Eurus for now. The backwater planet had little other reason to make most people stay, and so the Academic Institute station was mostly empty. Everything had been packed up and squared away, ready for business to resume once the weather allowed for it in a few months. But even with things here in the off season as it were, the station still maintained a small permanent population, of which Kellermann was a part. If home was where the heart is, then for him that was Eurus, and that was where he wanted to stay.

Kellermann had been expecting a quiet and uneventful day. Most of the research expedition's personnel had already left, leaving behind only the station's permanent crew, and booking for the station's scientific facilities wasn't due to begin 'til the end of the week. Even the business with the missing Artifact 93 had seen no progress. All Kellermann had to look forward to for the day was minor paperwork. He was gazing idly into space through his quarters' bay window, when his desk computer chimed. Whipped out of his distracted state, he glanced at the screen - it was the station commander - and accepted the call.

The commander's image appeared on screen. "Doctor Kellermann, we've received a priority message from the Solar Navy. I think you need to hear this."

Kellermann's immediate thought was of Artifact 93. "Very good, commander. Please, put it through."

The commander pressed a couple of buttons, and the message began playing.

"Eurus Science Station, this is an emergency message from SNV Durendal. A pirate vessel is en route to your location. We have alerted local Naval forces, but we cannot provide a reliable ETA for the pirates' arrival. We recommend immediate evacuation of the facility until armed support can arrive. Durendal out."

Kellermann furrowed his brow. "Pirates? Here? What in space could they want with us?"

"I don't know, sir, but I don't want to take any chances. I'm ordering all personnel to the emergency shuttles. Please make your way to the hangar bay."

Before Kellermann could reply, the commander terminated the message. A second later, the evacuation alarm began glaring. Kellermann sighed in exasperation, saved his work, and made his way out into the corridor, where a few other people were also hurrying for the shuttles. So much for a quiet day's work.

*   *   *

The atmosphere was tense in the station's command centre, if not on the verge of outright panic. With Eurus such a backwater, this sort of occurrence was all but unheard of, and even with evacuation drills no-one was fully prepared for the situation.

"Is the evacuation proceeding as planned?" the station commander asked, as much to break the tension as anything else.

"Yes, commander. Emergency supplies are all loaded, and all personnel are accounted for," an officer replied, just about managing to keep their voice level. "Shuttles one and two are away."

"Commander, there's a ship coming out of lightspeed. It's not broadcasting any recognition codes, and I don't have its profile on record... I-I think it's the pirates!"

Clearly visible through the command centre's panoramic windows, a lot closer than any other ship would approach, an old a battered starship emerged into normal space. It barely waited a second before it turned and flared its engines, flying alongside the station like a circling predator. As it flew, some of its weapon bays deployed and released their payload: rounded metallic objects a few metres across on each side, tumbling away from the ship at regular intervals.

"What's it doing?" the station commander demanded. "What are those?"

An officer checked their sensors. "Mines, commander. Looks like they plan to trap us."

True to the officer's guess, the mines were activating manoeuvring engines and moving to form a spherical web around the station. Within a minute or so, the station was completely surrounded by dozens of them. The ship lurked outside the sphere, guns trained on the station.

Across the entire facility, the PA system crackled to life. "Eurus Station, we've come for information on the Sagittarians. Hand over your top scientists and we won't open fire. You have five minutes to comply."

The commander stared at the ship for a moment, before reaching for the comm. "Pirate vessel, we have no intention of surrendering any material or personnel to you. Disarm your mines and leave at once."

"Negative, Eurus Station. We're not leaving until we get what we want. Hand over the scientists, or we will take them by force."

A call came in over an internal channel. "It's Professor Kellermann here. Commander, what exactly is going on out there?"

"The pirates have us trapped, sir. I assume you heard their demands?"

"I did, yes." There was a long silent pause. "Er, I take it the Navy is coming to help?"

"They've been alerted, Doctor. I'd guess that they'll be arriving any moment--"

"Commander, new ships incoming - they're Naval signatures!"

Sure enough, more ships were jumping in, bearing the livery of the Navy's Outer Fleet. As they aligned themselves to the station's orientation, the minefield responded automatically. A few dozen mines broke off formation and rocketed off towards the Navy ships. Once they were within range, the mines detonated, sending surges of chaotic electromagnetic energy raking across the ships of the flotilla, tearing through their systems. Engines guttered and went cold, lights flickered and died, gun turrets ground to a halt. The flotilla was disabled, drifting helplessly askew.

"Your would-be rescuers are dead in space, Eurus Station." The pirate message was much more smug this time, but no less threatening. "Don't count on the Navy coming to save you, we have plenty more EMP mines. I say again, hand over your top scientists. This doesn't need to get violent."

The seconds ticked by, silent, tense. Kellermann was pacing up and down an empty corridor. He knew that ultimately there was no choice about what had to be done. It was the right thing to do, it was the sensible thing to do. But he really didn't want to do it.

"Professor..."

"Yes, Commander, I know." He let out a tremendous sigh. "Tell them I'm on my way." With leaden feet, he made his way to the hangar bay, like a man being led to the gallows.

The hangar wasn't empty, but the area around shuttle three was distinctly bare. All the station's other personnel who were present were giving the ship a wide berth. They watched him nervously - Kellermann couldn't tell if they were expressing sympathy, or making sure he went through it. If it was the latter, they needn't have worried - Kellermann didn't pause as he trudged up the loading ramp and into the cockpit. He began the activation procedure, and as the shuttle came online and the berth doors opened, he gazed out into space. The pirate frigate loomed in the near distance. He suppressed another sigh and reached for the comm.

"Shuttle three to Station, taking her out now. Good luck."

"To both of us, Professor. Thank you."

With that, Kellermann lifted off the platform and took the shuttle out. He half expected the mines to go off and paralyse his ship as he passed them, but they remained inactive. As he approached the pirate vessel, he saw its own hangar doors open in anticipation of his arrival. The shuttle gave a sudden jerk as the frigate's tractor beams engaged and seized the shuttle, dragging it into the bay. As the shuttle touched down on the deck, the ramp extended on its own. If Kellermann's feet had been heavy before, now they seemed practically welded to the floor. Nonetheless, he mustered up the strength to make his way out of the ship, each step seemingly lasting an eternity, and eventually found himself standing on the flight deck. A host of disreputable-looking characters were there waiting for him, guns in their hand and suspicion in their faces.

As a few of them pushed past him to investigate the shuttle, one lifted a finger to their earpiece. "Scientist's here, Cap'n... aye, just the one. What d'you want done with him? ... aye-aye, Cap'n." The pirate lowered their hand and turned their attention back to Kellermann. "Captain Strannik wants to see you. Don't move."

Kellermann did his best to remain defiantly silent, but had to settle for timidity instead. As he waited for the captain, he couldn't help nervously eyeing up all the weapons the ship's crew were holding - one of them was tapping a finger impatiently against a trigger guard in a subtle yet profoundly unsettling way. Kellermann's gaze flicked up to the finger's owner's face, and he received a broad smirk that really didn't help his nervousness.

It was only a few minutes before the doors to the hangar opened, to admit two more pirates. The one in front carried himself with a dignified swagger that indicated by its boundless confidence that he was the one in charge. He strode up to Kellermann, regarding him with a carefully assembled expression of magnanimity.

"Welcome aboard the good ship Corsair, my esteemed friend!" he said by way of greeting, spreading his arms expansively. "My name is Captain Morgan Strannik, and I trust you'll forgive my crew and I our rather rough reception - you must understand that we're ill-adapted to receiving guests of your academic stature."

"I cannot honestly say it's been the most pleasant welcome I've ever had, Mister Strannik," Kellermann replied, his fear covered by a thin layer of frostiness. However refined the pirate's attitude might have been, he had the sneaking feeling that he was being mocked.

Strannik's cheek twitched at the "mister", but he ploughed on undaunted. "I can only apologise, of course. Please understand that we're common folk, not at all the fine people you must be used to rubbing shoulders with. Speaking of which, with who might I have the pleasure of speaking?"

"I am Professor Lorentz Kellermann," he announced, drawing himself up to his full height, which didn't quite measure up to Strannik's, "and I am a respected member of the Commonwealth Academic Institute."

"How very impressive, Professor. I gather you're an expert on the Sagittarians, too?"

"As it happens, yes I am."

"Perfect! That's what you're here for. Ankerak, prepare some labspace for our guest."

The scarred Ylerakk who had followed Strannik into the hangar saluted and hustled off. Kellermann narrowed his eyes at Strannik.

"What you seem to be missing is that I am a respected citizen of the Solar Commonwealth. They will be coming to rescue me."

"You mean like that Outer Fleet task group?" Strannik asked airily. "Y'know, the one currently lying dead and helpless in space out by Eurus Station?"

"There are other ships in the Commonwealth fleet, Mr. Strannik, and they will be coming for you."

"Then I'd suggest, Professor, that you work nice and quickly before that happens. And incidentally..." Strannik reached out and wrapped his fingers in Kellermann's lapels, pulling the archaeologist's face up to his own. "It's CAPTAIN Strannik."

*   *   *

The Wyvern arrived at Eurus first. As it settled into a stable orbit near the science station, Laszlo and Isis surveyed the scene. It was not a pretty sight - no-one in their line of work was terribly fond of the Navy - but under the circumstances an entire task group lying dead in the water was far from a welcome sight.

Laszlo was aghast - his Naval training told him that this was no mean feat. "Christ... how could Strannik have pulled this off?"

"He took us out with an EMP mine at Sel'Akis, remember?" Isis reminded him. "I guess he must have had some more mines to spare."

"Some?" Laszlo scoffed. "His hold must have been stuffed to the brim with them!" He glanced behind him, where Elgar was standing, and gestured vaguely out of the window. "Are you seeing this, Captain?"

"I am, Laszlo. Ms. Lagato is quite correct," he answered, deeply troubled, "a quick strike with a powerful EMP weapon could manage this. But how they did it isn't important right now - I need to talk to the station."

Laszlo nodded and stood up, gesturing to Elgar to take his place. The Captain sat down and turned to the comms console.

"Eurus Station, this is Captain Elgar Humboldt of the Solar Navy, requesting an immediate status report."

"This is Eurus Station, the situation is under control here... but that doesn't look like a Navy ship, "Captain"?"

"I've assumed temporary command of this civilian vessel in an emergency situation. I'm currently tracking a pirate called Morgan Strannik, and I have reason to believe he was there not long ago?"

"Well, there was certainly a pirate here. You've probably seen their handiwork - they've also abducted our chief scientist, Professor Lorentz Kellermann. We have the ship's departure vector - sending it over now."

Elgar looked up expectantly at Isis, but she only shook her head. "Won't do us much good. Even if Strannik knows where he's going, he's not going to jump straight there."

"Well, what do you suggest, then?"

"Those shards were Sagittarian tech, right? So maybe they're designed to interface with something..."

Elgar nodded as he picked up the thread of Isis's thinking, and turned back to the comm. "Eurus Station, can you give me a list of Sagittarian excavations with surviving technology present?"

"We can, Captain. Do you think those pirates are planning something?"

"It's a distinct possibility. Thank you for your help, Eurus - Captain Humboldt out." He glanced over his screen as the list came from Eurus Station, then switched comm channel. "Captain Humboldt to Durendal. What's the situation, Mx. Leurak?"

"Durendal here, Captain. We're helping to coordinate the repair efforts for the disabled flotilla. Rescue ships are incoming - shall we stay to assist?"

"Don't get too involved just yet, Commander. I have a feeling we may need to be on the move very soon. I'm sending over a list of Sagittarian sites with intact technology - we think Strannik will be heading for one of them."

"Acknowledged, Captain. Might I suggest sending a copy to Navy command, sir? The more ships we have at the ready, the sooner we can get any of these sites locked down."

"Good thinking, Commander. Proceed."

On the Durendal's bridge, Leurak turned xir gaze to the comms officer. "Ms. Torzay, do we have the list?"

"Yes, Commander, download is complete. Shall I open a channel to the Flagship?"

"Do it."

Torzay tapped at her console. "SNV Orion, this is the SNV Durendal. We have urgent information regarding an ongoing situation. Please respond."

It was only a second or two before a reply was forthcoming, as the helmetted visage of the Lord Admiral appeared in hologram before them, gazing imperiously at Commander Leurak.

"We read you, Durendal. Go ahead."

"Admiral, the Sagittarian shards have been stolen. They're in the possession of Morgan Strannik, and he's also kidnapped Professor Lorentz Kellermann to help decipher them."

"Damn." The centuries-old helmet that he habitually wore couldn't change expression to betray his feelings, but the Admiral was clearly not happy. "Do we have any idea where's he headed?"

"Not specifically, sir. But we obtained a list of Sagittarian excavation sites from Eurus Station - we assume he'll end up at one of them sooner or later."

"Very probably, I suppose," the Admiral said to himself, before once again addressing Leurak. "Alright, send the list over. We'll disseminate it to the rest of the Navy and seek permission for deployment. Await further instructions for now - this could get... interesting very soon."

Leurak saluted xir acknowledgment, and the Admiral dismissed the hologram. For a brief moment he simply sat in thought, gently tapping one hand on the arm of his throne-like command chair. Even seated, he was an imposing figure - a cyborg giant of a person wearing armour from head to toe, a system of powered plating that both clad and comprised his body.

"We've received the Durendal's list, Lord Admiral."

As the comms officer spoke, the Admiral turned his attention back to his bridge and rose to his heftily greaved feet. "Good. Send it to every ship we have and open a Navy-wide channel."

"Aye-aye, sir." The comms officer spent a few seconds carrying the order out, then gave a nod to the Admiral.

"Solar Navy, this is Lord Admiral Rigel speaking. We have an emerging situation that may require your action at a moment's notice. You are being sent a list of Sagittarian excavation sites, any of which could soon be the target of pirate attack. If you are within response range of any of these locations, go to battle readiness and stand by. If you receive orders to head to any of these locations and engage enemy presence, they override any other orders you may currently be carrying out. Orion out."

"Data sent, Admiral. All recipients acknowledging."

"Excellent. Put the Orion on alert status as well, and prepare the stardrive for immediate departure. Open a channel to the Galactic Palace - we may need full deployment permission. If something gets started, I intend to finish it."

*   *   *

This was not exactly the nicest working environment Professor Kellermann had ever worked in. The so-called "laboratory" that Morgan Strannik had provided him was just a disused storage room with a few lights and computer terminals brought in, and the ship had little in the way of proper scientific equipment to furnish it. Most of it had clearly been scrounged up from whatever sources these pirates could steal from, and some of it was of no archaeological use at all. Undoubtedly the worst part, though, was the Tygoethan thug standing guard. The repto-mammalian pirate hadn't stopped glaring at Kellermann since Strannik had assigned them their post, as if they were daring Kellermann to make a wrong move, and the way their thick fingers were drumming on their gun was rather distracting. It was far from the place Kellermann would have chosen to bring the three Sagittarian shards together. The great mystery of the Sagittarians deserved more auspicious surroundings, he felt, and it definitely deserved proper analysis equipment.

With one last nervous glance at the surly guard, Kellermann gave up on waiting for a miraculous rescue and turned his attention to the shards, sitting on a table against one wall. He pored over them for a moment - they were obviously three parts of a circular whole that had been cut apart at some point, with a blank surface on one side and worn, corroded access ports on the other - but there was little to be gleaned from just staring at them.

"Er, excuse me? W-Would you mind helping me with, er... ?" Kellermann addressed the guard and hesitantly indicated the shards. The guard just continued staring daggers at him, and Kellermann trailed off. He sighed and resigned himself to all doing the work himself. He lifted the shards each onto the table in the middle of the room - with some effort, given how large and heavy each one was - and arranged them in a circle, having carefully matched the circuitry patterns in the cut surfaces. He pushed each shard in towards the others and, grinding heavily across the metal table, they met each other for the first time in millions of years.

Nothing seemed to be happening. Kellermann stared at the shards, hoping for some insight in the complete trio, but it wasn't forthcoming. He frowned in thought, and glanced up at some of his equipment in the hopes that he might be able to find some use for it, when...

A sudden little sound from the shards. And was that movement?

Kellermann's gaze snapped back to the shards. They were indeed moving on their own! Before his eyes, they pulled themselves together into proper place, as the circuitry along each shard's edges extruded itself outward in strands and filaments. Prehensile metal reached out and meshed itself together, and pulled the body of the shards into place behind it. As the shards were pressed together, the seams between each piece filled in as though liquid were being poured into the space. Although slow to start after untold millennia, the self-repair systems worked quickly, and in less than a minute the three shards had joined into a single object.

Kellermann stood in amazement at the sight, but the Sagittarian artifact had one more trick up its sleeve. As the shards completed their reintegration, light began to bloom on its flat upper surface. Patterns of illumination drew themselves over the artifact, producing curved smears of light made up of an uncountable myriad of little points, their glow blended into each other by the density of their grouping.

For a brief instant, Kellermann simply marvelled at the sight, until somewhere in his excited thoughts was made the connection: stars! The artifact's light had produced what surely could only have been a representation of part of the Galaxy. It was focused on a different segment of it than the Commonwealth's Sol-centred cartography, but even then the shapes of the drifts of stars were familiar.

As Kellermann tried to guess at the identities of some of these stars, a wave of colour washed over the map as many of them turned green. Radiating out of one among the billions of motes, in an instant a green mass had formed across the map. Encircled within a solid line and annotated with strings of little alien letters, it could only have been the Sagittarian empire. Before Kellermann could fully take in the spectacle, the map started to turn an angry red. Every star seemed to be engulfed in holographic flames and was quickly consumed. In the blank space left as the map receded, a strange symbol appeared... or was it more than that? Its exact form wasn't immediately apparent, but between its horned, skull-like shape and the implications of the burned-away map, it was a decidedly unnerving sight.

The warped death's head leered eyelessly out from the artifact for a moment, before fading away and being replaced by the starmap again. It was uncoloured this time, but not unlabelled - one star on the edge of the map, lonely and isolated, was indicated. Strings of Sagittarian numerals were attached to its pointer - coordinates, no doubt - and a symbol appeared above it, depicting a circle containing curved lines. Kellermann guessed that this was a simplified representation of the very artifact he was looking at, and his guess was borne out as the symbol split into three wedges. Each wedge moved away from the marked star, deeper into the Galaxy, each tracing a line to a new star. As the wedges arrived at their destinations, those stars were marked just like the first.

Kellermann was staggered. This was by far the clearest message the Sagittarians had ever left behind, and he was probably the first person to see it since it was recorded! What was more, he knew exactly what it meant - or at least a very specific part of it. One of the stars that was still helpfully labelled, on the upspin edge of Sagittarian territory, he knew for a fact was orbited by a little planet he was very familiar with - Eurus. The other two labelled stars he didn't recognise immediately, but their positions matched the Academic Institute's best guess at the extent of Sagittarian territory. And each of these three locations was connected to a common origin point - Kellermann didn't recognise that star at all, but it was clearly significant...

"You found something, then?"

Kellermann nearly jumped out of his skin. He whipped around like a startled animal to see the guard looming over his shoulder, studying the hologram. Their gaze flicked back to the scientist, less unfriendly but still menacing.

"I, uh-- y-yes, I think so," Kellermann stammered, before steadying himself to continue. "Perhaps you ought to, ah, contact your captain and bring him down here. I imagine he'll want to see this."

The guard stepped back a little and brought a finger to their earpiece. They barked a report to whoever was on the other end of the line, bringing them up to speed on Kellermann's progress.

What neither they nor Kellermann knew was that this wasn't the only message being sent. Clinging to the artifact's surface, dispersed into a discreet swarm of nanoscopic units, someone else had seen the Sagittarian recording, and was even now relaying the news to its own contact...

Chapter 11

The waiting was the worst part. This was not the first major interstellar threat the Lord Admiral had been involved in, and the pattern was all too familiar: a long period of anxious tension that alternated between bursts of frantic but decisive action and painfully prolonged stretches of helpless waiting. It was all he could do not to pace up and down the bridge just to occupy himself - he knew it wouldn't make him feel any better, and it would probably make the rest of the bridge crew feel worse.

He was making do with reviewing the Orion's diagnostic readout - nothing on it needed his particular attention, but it kept his thoughts occupied - when a message came through on his private channel. He checked the sender, and it was exactly what he'd been waiting for.

"Rigel,

Sagittarian shards reactivated - displayed message, starmap. Can't broadcast tracking signal - too easily detected - but can send map. Strannik likely heading straight there.

- Mat"

Rigel called up the attached file, and watched the last message of the Sagittarians. Much like Kellermann he was impressed by the sense of history's weight it embodied, but unlike Kellermann he was much more familiar with the geography of the Galaxy, and could recognise the highlighted stars. He brought up a more modern map of the Galaxy and checked the origin star in Commonwealth listings. Its entry was a brief one - a minor star in the unregarded backwater of the Bastion Province, home to a couple of tiny planets and a lot of spacedust, with no resources worth the trouble of travelling that far off the beaten path. It had only received a cursory sweep from a Galactic Survey exploration mission, which had detected alien ruins on the surface but had declared them a minor curiosity at best, being too small and buried to be of much interest. With the Interregnum having broken out only a few days after the sweep, it was no wonder that the system had been all but forgotten.

But that had been decades ago, in a very different time. Today that system could very well have been the most important system in the Commonwealth, if not the entire Galaxy.

"Helm, we have a new heading!" Lord Admiral Rigel stood up and sent the star's coordinates to the bridge systems. "Set course for this star, maximum speed. Comms, contact the First Fleet and have them marshal at those coordinates, and alert the Bastion Province Fleet to the situation."

"Aye-aye, Admiral!"

As the mighty flagship charged its engines for the journey and sent out its command, Rigel settled back into his seat, a weight of tension taken off his shoulders. Even if the FTL jump meant more waiting, it was at least waiting with a definite goal.

*　　*　　*

GS-KV-649 was a big name for such a minor system. So far from even the sparsely distributed population of the Commonwealth's Bastion Province, only a few stars' distance from the edge of the Milky Way, it was one of those systems that seemed to exist just to fill in the blank spaces on the starmap. Warships of the First Fleet were already filtering in at the Lord Admiral's command, the nearest and the fastest all assembling in orbit of the larger and closer of the little yellow star's planets, and it was by far the busiest the system had been for uncounted millennia.

The Durendal dropped in, joining the rest of the fleet. Standard Naval procedure after an FTL jump was to immediately establish sensor coverage of the area, but with so many Navy ships already here it was hardly necessary. The first handful of ships to arrive had launched wings of Sabre-class scoutfighters to recon the system, giving the system the most in-depth mapping it had probably ever seen.

"Raven Leader to SNV Britain, beginning flyover of outer planet."

"Roger, Raven Leader. Any sign of the target?"

"Negative, Britain. We're alone out here."

"Anything on the planet's surface?"

"Raven 4 to Britain, I've got something. Looks like an artificial structure - a facility of some kind."

"Describe it for us, Raven 4."

"Taking her down for a closer look... it's a small facility, built into a cliffside. Overlooking a crater of some kind."

"Impact zone?"

"Doesn't look like it, Britain - the shape is too regular. And there's a network of some sort built underneath it..."

"Raven 5 to Britain, we've got a ship incoming! Frigate class, not broadcasting any ID!"

"It must be Strannik! SNV Britain to First Fleet, target has entered the system! Moving to intercept!"

*   *   *

There wasn't much time. Morgan Strannik knew that for all the Commonwealth's faults, they wouldn't hesitate to defend what they thought was theirs. Once the Corsair arrived in the system, they would need to move quickly. To that end, Strannik and Kellermann were already sitting in one of the Corsair's shuttles, along with the artifact and a team of pirates. The rumble of the shuttle's engines reverberated through the little craft, ready to launch the moment the word was given.

Strannik didn't quite know what to make of the artifact's message. He wasn't unintelligent, but apparently he lacked the context that Kellermann had. The professor had been absolutely thrilled - a drastic change from his previous state of terrified defiance - and had told Strannik at length about his findings with surprising enthusiasm. A lot of it had gone over Strannik's head, but the message itself had been fairly clear. It hadn't excited him nearly as much as it had Kellermann.

Rather, it had given him an uneasy knot in the pit of his stomach. A leering skull burning away a third of the galaxy was a foreboding sight by anyone's standards, and it gave Strannik the horrible feeling that he was meddling in things way above his paygrade, getting himself in way too deep.

"Coming up on KV-649 now, Captain."

But even if the thought of backing down had ever crossed his stubborn mind, crossing the very threshold of the star system was far too late to be having doubts. Strannik moved through the shuttle and ducked into the cockpit.

"Are we ready to get underway?" he asked.

"Aye, sir," the pilot replied, not glancing up from the controls, "as soon as the hangar doors open, we can head out."

"Good. We'll probably be under Navy fire the moment we drop into realspace, so don't screw this up."

With that, Strannik returned to the passenger cabin and resumed his seat. He fixed his gaze upon Kellermann, who had returned to his sullen terror amidst the several heavily-armed pirates.

"So, Professor, once we reach the planet we're heading for, what will we need to find?"

Kellermann looked up from the artifact and stared at Strannik for a long moment, before drawing a resigned breath. "I don't know exactly, but I imagine there'll be Sagittarian ruins on the planet's surface. If the artifact has anything more to tell us, it'll likely interface with whatever technology is still there."

"Assuming they haven't already been picked clean by now," one of the pirates rumbled half to themselves.

"This system was charted only a few days before the Interregnum began, and the Academic Institute could only cover so much ground even after it ended. This system is so remote I doubt even your, ah, peers will have gotten to it yet."

There was no mistaking the acid in Kellermann's words, but a glance from Strannik silenced any response. There was no time for any further argument anyway, as the metaspace exit alert sounded throughout the ship, audible even inside the shuttle.

Strannik's head darted up at the sound. "Get us underway, pilot!" he shouted at the cockpit, but it wasn't necessary - the shuttle was already lifting off the deck and pushing forward out of the hangar. The pirates all half-expected to come under fire from the Navy at any moment, but it wasn't coming just yet.

By deft navigation the Corsair had arrived low over KV-649-2, on the very edge of its sparse, shallow atmosphere, and the Britain and its scouts were too high up to go on an immediate offensive.

"Captain, we're getting a lot of Navy comm chatter from the inner planet," Ankerak warned via comm. "The Corsair can't hold its own against that cruiser, let alone an entire fleet."

"Take her out of the system for now," replied Strannik, "and use a random FTL vector. We can handle things from here - keep a channel open just in case, though."

The Corsair turned away from the planet as it prepared for another FTL jump, and the shuttle continued down towards its surface. It was a rough, craggy landscape of grey rock and dust, shaped by millions of years of meteoric activity and whatever feeble tectonic activity the little planet could muster. Hundreds of miles of unimpressive terrain encircled the little planet, save for the single point of interest it could boast, which the shuttle flew quickly towards.

Set into a wide cliff range were a number of observation windows and open hangar bays, overlooking a vast crater. True to Raven 4's assessment, it did not look like a simple impact crater - the floor and walls looked as though they had been scoured smooth when they had formed, save for a few patches of torn-up ground. Protruding edges were all drawn inwards, trails of teased-out rock all pointing in to one shared centre. Looking more closely at the crater, it seemed as if some powerful force had reached out and scooped out a large, perfectly round area of the planet.

The occupants of the shuttle had barely a moment to take this all in, as the ship coasted over the scene and into the cliff's central hangar. As soon as the loading ramp lowered, Strannik and his crew hustled out in spacesuits, Kellermann trailing behind them.

The hangar was in a sorry state. It was a rough, bare-bones facility that had been built purely for function over style, and the millions of years since its use had not been kind. Layers of grit and dust covered various surfaces and a lot of its machinery had decayed, lying ruined here and there. But stranger than that was a pattern of damage to the entire bay - some of the floor panels had been torn out of place, and the overall structure appeared warped and distended. Much like the crater it overlooked, the facility seemed to have been pulled by some incredible force.

Kellermann noticed all this with his trained eye, but the pirates didn't pay it any attention. They spread out to secure the bay, rifles at the ready, but the place had been cleared out aeons ago. No physical threats were present, just an eerie graveyard aura that hung over the place.

Strannik turned to Kellermann. "Alright Professor, what are we looking for?"

"Er, well... the artifact seems to be part of a larger system, so there will likely be something missing. Probably the primary computer. I imagine that will be deeper in the facility, but it's a small base, so..."

Strannik swept his gaze across the hangar, and saw the wide doors at the back of the bay. Thinking this a likely guess, he pointed his crew in their direction and strode with them in the low gravity over to the doorway. There was no hope of restoring power to the ancient systems in the short time they had, so Strannik ordered two of the pirates to cut the door open. Their heavy combat rifles had been issued by Strannik with circumstances like this specifically in mind - there were a lot of storage vaults and lockdown doors in their line of work - and the pirates knew exactly what to do. The pair hefted their guns, and a blue-hot beam of plasma shot out of each one. The alloy of the doors gradually heated up, first red, then yellow, then white, as the pirates traced out an aperture big enough to admit them. Molten slag sloughed off in layers as the plasma slowly cut through, until finally a tall square section had been carved free. The pirates released their rifles' triggers and the actinic blue of the cutting beams vanished to leave only the amber glow of molten metal.

Strannik stepped up and gave the severed panels a hefty kick, shoving them out of the doors' track and opening the way forward. Inside was a short corridor with an identical set of doors at the other end. The team carved through these in the same way as the first, and found something beyond them.

"Aha..." Strannik muttered half to himself, "this looks promising!"

Inside the room was a circle of four large modules, covered with long-dead screens and intricate circuitry. Even with the divide in technological architecture between the Sagittarians and modern civilisation, it was easy to recognise these ancient machines as supercomputers. Each one stood as tall as any of them, but even they were dwarfed by the unit in the centre. If these were indeed computers, then a system of this size must have had processing power of astounding capacity. But most interesting of all was a circular cavity in the main unit, with bare circuitry in it surfaces and an inner edge that looked distinctly as though something had been cut out.

"Looks like we've found what we're looking for. Bring the artifact in here."

Two of the pirates hurried back to the shuttle to retrieve the artifact, returning in short order with the ancient disc carried between them. They held it up to the cavity and studied the inner surfaces, trying to match the patterns of circuitry along both objects' rims. They spun the artifact around as they did, before they were finally satisfied by its orientation and pressed it into place. The artifact slid smoothly into the cavity and settled in place like the final piece of a jigsaw puzzle. There was a pause, heavy with anticipation, as everyone gathered waited to see what, if anything, would happen...

There was stillness for a moment, as if the ancient machinery was considering its options, then a slight twitch as the artifact shifted in its socket, turning a few degrees to properly line itself up. The seam between artifact and socket began to fill up, as if metal were being poured in from some unknown source. In seconds, the artifact looked as though it had never left this place.

At the moment that the seam had fully sealed itself, there was a gentle tremor underneath everyone's feet. It was little more than a twitch, not enough to move anything, but something was definitely happening. In the ceiling, a couple of lights flickered fitfully as power flowed into them for the first time in untold millennia. The computer also lit up, a myriad of little lights blinking into life as the system resumed long-paused processes. In a haze of green static, a holographic screen resolved itself over the surface of the artifact. Lines of little Sagittarian glyphs scrolled rapidly past as the operating system booted up.

Before anyone could do anything with the computer, a video began playing on the screen. An arthropodal being looked back from across millions of years at Kellermann and the gathered pirates. Its two primary eyes were focused on the recording device apparently being held in its hand, while secondary eyes lower on the sides of its head faced outward and idly tracked whatever was around the insectoid alien. Filamentous antennae curled and twitched behind its head, as one of the creature's four hands swept over them like someone fixing their hair, and its tripartite mouth opened to produce a series of clicks, trills, and buzzing noises.

Strannik tore himself away from the recording and turned to Kellermann. "Is that a Sagittarian, Professor?"

Kellermann still stared at the video, enraptured. "It... it must be..." came his hushed reply. "This is incredible!"

"Do you have any idea what they're saying?"

Kellermann shrugged and shook his head. "None whatsoever. This is the first time I've ever heard any spoken Sagittarian dialect... the first time anyone has for millennia, I should think. But they must feel very strongly about something - look at the way they're gesticulating, the way they emphasise certain phonemes..."

True to Kellermann's interpretation, the alien was speaking in a rather insistent manner. Whatever point they were trying to make, it was clearly a very important one.

"... this must be a warning. Whatever this facility was, it must have had something to do with the Extinction, and this person is trying to make sure that anyone stumbling across it doesn't make the same mistake they did." Kellermann turned to Strannik. "Mr. Strannik, I must insist that we turn back at once."

Even through the opaque visor of his helmet, Strannik's incredulity was obvious. "Turn back?! Like hell I will! Need I remind you, Professor, that the Navy is up there waiting for us?"

Kellermann drew himself up to his full height. "Mr. Strannik, what we have uncovered here goes far beyond whatever petty brigandry you've engaged in! If we stumble blindly about here without due care, we could bring down a catastrophe Humanity has never before seen, and I cannot in good conscience allow you to--"

Strannik soon tired of Kellermann's umbrage. He muted his channel to Kellermann and gestured dismissively in the direction of the shuttle. One of his crew obediently seized the professor and dragged him out of the computer room, yelling all the way.

"Right, now that he's out of the way," Strannik said to himself, rubbing his hands together, "let's see about opening this tomb..." He stepped up to the screen, where the alien's video had just stopped playing and closed. In its place, a user interface had appeared, with several buttons labelled in Sagittarian arrayed before Strannik. None of the words meant anything to him, nor indeed was the general layout terribly familiar, but he did his best to navigate the system nonetheless. It was slow going, but bit by bit he was able to tease out an underlying logic. He didn't know what he was accessing, but he knew he was accessing something.

The pirate who had dragged Kellermann away earlier stepped up to Strannik's side. "Captain, I checked the shuttle's sensors just now. A Commonwealth fleet is massing in orbit, and dropships are on the way. We'll probably dealing with an attack any minute now."

"Fine. Be ready for when that happens. I think I've almost got something..." Strannik continued trying to operate the computer. Whether by some breakthrough in his work or by lucky guess, he finally opened up a promising readout. The screen displayed a technical diagram of something round, with a number of annotations that seemed to indicate that it was mostly in good repair. Strannik smiled to himself, fancying that he'd found the controls to a door of some kind. As he searched the program for a button to open it, his mind conjured up thoughts of the riches that might lie within, and the wealth and power that would come flowing his way when he plundered it.

Soon enough, a likely-looking text box popped up. It was pulsing an important-looking orange colour, and the glyphs were larger and bolder than others. But whether Strannik recognised the message as a warning or not, he ignored it and pressed the button he assumed said "Open".

For a couple of tense seconds, nothing seemed to happen. Then a low rumble spread under the pirates' feet. The lights started to flicker, and some of the base's exposed systems shot out sparks. The computer's screen was rattling off an incessant progression of glyphs, too fast to be discerned. The pirates looked all around, but no-one had any idea what was happening. They looked to their captain - Morgan also didn't know what was going on, but he was more decisive about it. He exited the computer room and headed back to the hangar entrance, his crew following in his wake. He stopped at the deck's edge, where Kellermann was already standing, but no-one paid him any attention compared to what was happening below.

Around the rim of the crater, scattering rock and dust out of their way, a series of pylons rose from the ground, with clockwork smoothness despite the machinery's age. Lights flickered on their surfaces as ancient and arcane systems within came online for the first time in millennia. Some pylons took longer than others to rouse themselves to working order, but as each one did its lights began pulsing regularly, joining in with the rhythm of its neighbours. As the last of the pylons slid into place, the lights ceased pulsing and began to glow solidly. A disturbance started to form in the centre of the circle - space itself seemed to be rippling, sending light scattering in strange ways. Growing from the infinitesimal, a black point appeared in the midst of the emanating warp, expanding slowly but steadily. It was spherical, but with no details it was difficult to discern anything about the lightless circle, save that it was still getting bigger.

Morgan was at a complete loss, but looking at the orb made him distinctly uneasy. He looked around as if he might find answers in the hangar's doorway, and his gaze fell upon Professor Kellermann. Remembering the man for the first time since having him dragged away, he unmuted the channel.

"Er, Professor... any insight into all this?"

"What makes you think I have any idea?" Kellermann snapped back.

"Well, you're the Sagittarian expert!"

"This place has been lost for millennia, Strannik, and we're probably the first people to find it in that time... and you went and opened it up without a second thought. Well done."

"But what is that thing?! What's going on?!"

"I have no idea, but I'm sure we're going to find out..."

*   *   *

The SNV Orion was the flagship of the Solar Navy and it wore the title on its sleeve. Whenever it entered the area, it was obvious to anyone watching that this was an important ship, if for no other reason than it was absolutely huge. It stretched thirty kilometres from prow to stern, and it was more heavily armed and armoured than any other warship in the known Galaxy. Its presence was undoubtedly the most commanding of command ships.

The Orion arrived in space high above KV-649-2, its immense engines immediately setting about establishing a stable orbit. The rest of the First Fleet arrayed itself beneath, the last few stragglers jumping in to take their positions.

"So what's the situation?" the Lord Admiral asked, rising from his seat and striding to the edge of the balcony that overlooked the Orion's command centre.

"Strannik got here before us, Admiral. They made it to the ruins before the Fleet could muster, and they've... opened something."

"Something? What does that mean?"

The officer gave a shrug. "Unknown, sir. The facility is producing an anomalous object - it matches nothing on record."

"Bring it up on sensors."

An image of the black orb appeared above the central holoprojector. Even with the Fleet's birds-eye view, it was no less mysterious to them as it was to Strannik and his crew.

Rigel peered at the image, perplexed. "It's not giving off any kind of radiation? No gravity well?"

"No, sir. Sensors scans almost look like there's space inside it, as if it's some sort of opening, but the readings we're getting are distorted. It's difficult to make out what we're looking at."

Rigel considered the situation. If the anomaly was indeed an opening, then it seemed that this "tomb" was no mere memorial. There was space therein - compressed, somehow? A pocket dimension? - and something could well be buried inside. But Sagittarian was a difficult language to translate and "tomb" was only a best guess. And even if "Wargod" had a more benign translation, had it truly been buried here? Had it instead been dumped, or abandoned, or imprisoned?

This place is not a place of honour.

But the genie was out of the bottle. Strannik had reactivated this thing, whatever it was, and even if they chased him off he and his crew wouldn't stay quiet about it. News would get out that the Wargod's Tomb was real, and people would come looking. This needed to be dealt with sooner or later, and when would be a better time than with the entire First Fleet in orbit?

"The anomaly has stabilised, sir, its growth has ceased. Still no other readings."

"Which ship is closest to the surface?"

"The cruiser Ajax, sir. Shall I put them through?"

Rigel gave a nod, and the hologram of the anomaly was quickly replaced with the image of the Ajax's commanding officer, who snapped off a salute.

Rigel returned the gesture. "Commodore Singh, what's your status?"

"All systems are nominal, Lord Admiral," the commodore answered. "We're scanning the anomaly, but I can't imagine we're getting anything more than the Orion. What are your orders, sir?"

"Launch a sensor probe into the anomaly to get a closer look. Relay all its data to the Orion - whatever is in there, I want to know it is."

"At once, sir." Commodore Singh gave a silent nod to her executive officer, who immediately set about carrying the command out. In less than a minute, the sensor probe came rocketing out of one of the Ajax's missile tubes. As its manoeuvring thrusters deployed it turned to face the anomaly and fired its engines to head towards it. In rapid sequence its various sensor systems all came online, regarding its mysterious and ever-approaching goal with virtually every form of electronic analysis known to the Commonwealth. The probe's systems registered the anomaly as empty space - the spherical entity was like a three-dimensional hole, and the probe deftly threaded the needle as it entered the strange portal.

The inner space seemed thoroughly empty - without even the weak light or sparse dust of KV-649, it was a black pit of pure nothingness. With nothing immediate to see, the probe slowed down and began emitting sensor waves in the hope of finding something. Part of the waves bounced back. The probe focused its attention in that direction, and detected a thick, dense surface. Its contours were not those of an asteroid or some other chunk of space debris - they were clearly artificial. Beneath it, a faint glimmer of energy began moving through it. The probe's scanning beams had woken something up.

As if in answer to the probe, the thing beneath it sent up its own sensor beam. It studied the probe, laid its shape bare, saw all the way through it - and past it, to the opening into normal space that the probe was broadcasting into, and through which came trickling back the background radiation of an inhabited universe. For the first time in too long, the thing heard and saw something, and deep in its thoughts resolved to meet it head-on.

As the probe watched, the thing began to move with surprising speed, unheeding of the little machine before it. The probe's last moments were of the sight of that thick, dense surface rapidly drawing closer, before--

Rigel leant forward in his seat as the bridge's holo-image turned to static. He raised the Ajax on comms.

"Commodore, is there a problem?"

"We've lost the feed from the anomaly, sir," Singh replied. "I think we've lost the probe altogether - whatever it found is coming out."

The Lord Admiral patched in the rest of the fleet. "Rigel to First Fleet, go to yellow alert. Prepare to meet unknown alien vessels."

As the ships of the First Fleet drew back from it, the anomaly began to change. What had once seemed to be merely an empty hole in space started to look more like a strange lens, as the details of some unknown object began to shift and roil through it like a bizarre kaleidoscope. Those who happened to look at the sphere found it playing tricks on their eyes, with depth and distance within it seeming quite at odds with its fairly small size. Like a sudden new perspective on an optical illusion, what appeared to be an orb only a few dozen metres across suddenly seemed to be a window on an area hundreds of kilometres deep.

What happened then defied any rational understanding of the nature of space. Something emerged from the anomaly, slowly and ponderously, as miles upon miles of metal unfurled impossibly into space. It almost seemed as though a contracted area of space and matter was being turned inside out, returning to normal shape after having been folded up, but no-one watching was really in any state to puzzle the concept out. Especially since the nature of the thing itself was becoming all too clear.

"Admiral, I'm detecting energy readings throughout the object. They're running through a network, clearly artificial... the energy is concentrating itself in a lot of surface emplacements... Admiral, I think this thing is a starship. More to the point, it's a very heavily-armed starship."

The object's architecture was alien in its details, but now that the shock of its disgorgement into space had died down its basic form was quite recognisable. It was a vast structure of metal armour, tapering slightly inward toward the front from an immense aft section that bore a complex of massive engines, which were flaring at full burn to lift the mighty vessel into a stable orbit. From either side of the aft projected a pair of extensions that curved forward, the front-facing conical sections composed of nestled tubes that were unmistakably guns. The surfaces of the ship were riddled with even more weapons, from serried ranks of point defense batteries to missile banks like mountain ranges to cannons the length of cities. In the vessel's underside and creeping up its flanks were openings into large inner spaces, in which lights were flickering to life.

On every Commonwealth ship in the system, everyone near a window or a display stared at the immense machine in astonishment. Though their feelings about it were varied, almost everyone felt some variation of dread. Even the Lord Admiral, as old as he was, had never seen anything like this. Its size alone was worrying enough - three hundred kilometres long, it utterly dwarfed the Orion - but between that and the sheer mass of weaponry it possessed, this ship was a very clear statement of intent. Nothing this heavily armed was constructed with peaceful purposes in mind, except perhaps the peace of a graveyard.

"We're receiving a transmission from that thing, Admiral," the comms officer said before anyone could do anything further. "I don't recognise the data protocol, but I think I can... yes, here we go. Putting it through now."

The message was all but incomprehensible. The language being spoken - one of clicks, trills, and buzzing noises - was completely foreign to anyone listening, and the Orion's translation software was at a loss. But the tone of what was being said was less opaque. It was spoken evenly, dispassionately, with a sense of resolution to it. Not exactly upset, but definitely not happy either.

"What is the ship doing now?" the Admiral asked. Something about the message gave him a very bad feeling.

"It's turning to face the Fleet, sir. I'm picking up more sensor readings, smaller this time - more ships, I think--"

"Ajax to Orion, the alien ship's weapons have gone live! Missiles inbound!"

"Orion to First Fleet, red alert! Raise shields and prepare to return fire!"

As the ships of the First Fleet raised shields against the first volleys and moved into combat positions to fire their own, the alien dreadnought began to climb to meet them. Plasma bolts splashed against its powerful shields as smaller ships of similar architecture emerged from its underside hangar space and moved into battle.

The Wargod was awake. And it was angry.

Chapter 12

At the Durendal's maximum FTL speed, it was only a few hours' flight from Eurus to KV-649. Laszlo and Isis had spent that time clearing their belongings out of the Wyvern and piling it up in the cargo bay. Because the Durendal didn't have time to drop them off somewhere, Captain Humboldt had generously allowed them to remain aboard the Wyvern until the situation had stabilised. They were having one last meal aboard the ship that had been their home for years, in the galley with a bottle of rare wine sharing bittersweet reminisces, when the lights of the hangar turned red and alarms began going off.

Startled by the sudden red alert, Laszlo turned to Isis. "Looks like the First Fleet's caught up with the Corsair."

Isis continued staring out of the galley's large window. "Maybe... I dunno. Something feels wrong."

"What d'you mean? Wrong how?"

"I don't know, but... I just feel like things are about to get really ugly."

An experienced pirate like Laszlo learned never to dismiss an instinct like this, just in case it was right. He stood up from the table and stepped over to the comm screen on the wall.

"Wyvern to hangar control, what's going on? Why the red alert?"

"Control to Wyvern. Something big just appeared and is making hostile approach on the Fleet. Remain in dock and stand by for further instructions."

Laszlo and Isis were both perturbed. For all their professionalism, there had been a note of panic in the hangar technician's voice, which a ship like the Corsair shouldn't have merited.

"D'you think maybe Strannik called in a few favours, got a fleet together?" Laszlo asked more out of hope than anything else, as a knot of worry formed in his stomach.

Isis shook her head. "This quickly? I doubt it. And I can't see Strannik being able to pull together a pirate armada big enough to get a Navy officer that rattled. No, this must be very bad indeed."

The knot in Laszlo's gut tightened a little. He turned and left the galley without another word, Isis following him after draining her glass. As he stepped into the cockpit, Laszlo called up the Wyvern's sensor display. Dozens of ships surrounded them and the Durendal, milling around in what Laszlo and Isis both recognised as combat formation. Laszlo zoomed the map out, until the display showed them...

"... what the hell is that?!"

The two of them stared at the shape projected in hostile red on the sensor map, far bigger than anything else around it.

"They did it," said Laszlo in a hollow voice, "that bastard's only gone and done it. He's opened the bloody Tomb."

"So... it's real? That's the Wargod?"

"It must be. And it looks like it's brought friends..." Laszlo pointed out more enemy readings clustered below the Wargod. They were of much less monstrous size than the Wargod itself, ranging from fighter-shaped blips to the size of cruisers, but there were a lot of them. Alone, a fleet that size could probably match the First Fleet easily, but they very much weren't alone.

"Looks like you were absolutely right, Isis. Things are going to get really ugly."

*   *   *

The First Fleet of the Solar Navy had a formidable past, having been the driving force behind the defeat of the General's mechanised fleets during the Interregnum, but the Wargod was an equally formidable foe. Moving to encircle the alien behemoth in a hemispherical formation, none of the Commonwealth warships dared get within range of its main weapons, lest they join the wreckage that its opening salvos had already created. Its longer-ranged weapons lashed out at the nearest ships, missiles and mass accelerators chipping away at the fleet's shields. The fleet was responding in kind, but between the Wargod's shields, point-defense systems, and thick armour, they weren't making a scratch in the thing.

This would have been bad enough were it not a mere backdrop to the main battle. The ships that the Wargod had deployed were no less deadly than their Commonwealth counterparts - despite being millions of years old, the armada's technology was at least as advanced as the modern standard, and they also possessed the legendary Sagittarian self-repair tech that had preserved the Empire's ruins. Any ship disabled was only a temporary relief, as armour patched itself up and systems restored themselves. Even the wreckage of destroyed fighter drones had been reported gravitating back into shape and roaring to life once again. To add insult to injury, these weren't the only ships the First Fleet had to worry about. Even as they threw themselves full-tilt into the fray, more and more alien vessels were joining the battle. A slow but steady stream of reinforcements came trickling into the engagement, turning dozens of ships into hundreds. Recon flights showed the skeletons of new warships being rapidly fleshed out in the Wargod's massive hangar, assembled and launched in record time - every Sagittarian ship that was destroyed was due to be replaced manyfold, like the heads of a Hydra.

The First Fleet was not completely defenseless, though. Between the hard-won experience of its veterans and the cutting-edge training of its rookies, the Fleet was outmanoeuvring the enemy. For as many weapons as the Sagittarian armada had, combat analysis suggested that they were being guided by only one entity - data was being constantly broadcast from the Wargod itself to many of its subordinates. The larger ships that seemed to be under direct control were slower to react than Commonwealth ships and only got more so with every newcomer to the battle. Whoever or whatever was directing the Wargod's forces could only handle so much of the conflict by itself, leaving less important ships to default to an onboard intelligence that left something to be desired, especially against the elite personnel that made up the First Fleet's crews.

But it was all too clear to the Lord Admiral that this was eventually going to turn into a numbers game. The Wargod was as much a factory as a warship and its assembly lines were showing no signs of slowing down. If it remained content to hang back and leave the fighting to its puppets, the First Fleet would be ground down and ultimately defeated by attrition. Reinforcements from the Bastion Fleet would only prolong the conflict, not end it, and Rigel feared that summoning them would only convince the Wargod to join the battle itself. If it did, it could probably annihilate both fleets in a matter of minutes. Rigel did his best to keep the thought at bay, but he feared that nothing in the Galaxy could stop this thing.

With the fierce battle raging around them, no-one paid much attention as the command centre's doors opened, even though the person who stepped through them usually turned heads wherever she went. A full two metres tall, she carried herself with the kind of self-assuredness that could only come from being made of two tons of dense metal alloy. Although basically human-shaped, she was built in the image of some primordial reptilian super-predator - a thick tapering tail hung behind her and swung from side to side as she walked, her feet bore a pair of vicious sickle claws as big as a person's hand, and her head was a stout angular muzzle that, when she had cause to open her mouth, would reveal a set of knife-like teeth. She didn't need to be armed to look dangerous, but the bandoliers and beltwork strapped about herself had room for enough weapons to arm an entire squad.

She strode up to the Lord Admiral's chair and waited just behind it. Rigel glanced up from his holo-displays at the distinct sound of her footfalls and nodded in greeting.

"Ah, Artemis." He stood up to shake his old friend's hand. "Thanks for coming up here."

"I'm always happy to help, Admiral," Artemis replied, "and it looks like you need all the help you can get right now."

"Indeed," said Rigel, calling up a hologram of the Wargod. "So, what do you make of this?"

Artemis's eyes were just red light projected on the panels through which her optical sensors looked out, and her mouth had no articulation with which to smile or frown, so her options for expression were limited. Nonetheless, her concern at the image of the alien dreadnought was obvious. She crossed her arms across her chest and drummed her fingers thoughtfully.

"It's hard to know what to think of it," she said after a moment's thought. "A ship like this is virtually unprecedented. It almost reminds me of the first time I saw the Orion... but a lot bigger. And nastier."

"On the whole, I think I like the Orion better," Rigel grumbled. "This thing is building warships as fast as we can destroy them, and on its own it's all but untouchable. We can't keep fighting forever, so I need a solution and I need it now."

"If it's building ships, that suggests a weak point - unarmoured areas open to space." Artemis began pointing to places on the hologram. "The shipyard complex needs materials to build ships, so there may well be resource intakes. If they run deep enough into the ship, a strike at those areas may be enough to cripple it."

Rigel shook his head. "But what do we have that's powerful enough to deal enough damage? Even if we break through its shields, we'd likely need to focus fire in one location for quite a while, and its armada won't let us just sit there and blast it."

Artemis pondered for a second or two. "I think," she said quietly, "perhaps it's time to dip into the General's "private reserve"."

"Th-- ?!" Rigel was momentarily taken aback. But it looked like today was finally the day. "Very well. I suppose we don't have much choice. But what about getting it into place? If we load it into a missile, the Wargod will just shoot it down."

"I've thought of that too," Artemis replied. "Where is the Wyvern now?"

"The Wyvern? As far as I know, it should still be docked on the Durendal. Let's see if that's still the case..." Rigel sat back down and opened a channel. "Orion to Durendal. Are you receiving me?"

"We read you, Admiral. Your orders?" Captain Humboldt's voice was terse and his expression was cold and focused - in the heat of battle he had turned to the cold steel resolution that had won him his captaincy.

"We have a plan to deal with this thing, Captain, but we need the Wyvern for it. Is it still aboard?"

"It is, Admiral, but we can't spare any pilots to fly it."

"What about Hadron and Lagato?"

Humboldt furrowed his brow. "Well, they're still aboard too, sir, but are you sure that would be wise? Might they not just run?"

"I'm taking a gamble on their good nature. Put them through."

Elgar raised the Wyvern's frequency, and the call was soon accepted. "Las, Isis - there's someone who'd like to speak with you."

"Must be pretty urgent if-- oh!" Laszlo was taken aback by his company. Virtually everyone in the Commonwealth knew who Rigel was, and Laszlo was no exception. "Uh, hello Lord Admiral. To what do we owe the pleasure?"

"Hello, Mr. Hadron, Ms. Lagato. Have you been made aware of the alien dreadnought that just appeared?"

"Oh don't worry, we're aware," Laszlo answered, gesturing to the large red presence of the Wargod on the Wyvern's sensor map.

"I really hope you have some idea of what to do about that thing," Isis added as she leant into view.

"As it happens, we do," confirmed Rigel, "but we need your help to pull it off."

"What's the job?"

"Simply put, Ms. Lagato: find a way inside that monstrosity, plant the largest bomb we can give you on something important, and get out of there before it goes off."

"Well, it's a nice simple brief at least," Laszlo surmised with a shrug.

"And how exactly do you propose we get close enough to something that can hold off the entire First Fleet to do that?" Isis continued.

"Our hope is that the Wargod won't be able to see through the Wyvern's cloaking systems. And we'll have two battlegroups covering your approach, and lowering its shields long enough for you to get through."

"That's a risky strategy," Laszlo said, "a lot of people could be killed."

That is true, Mr. Hadron. But if we can't neutralise that thing, they'll probably be killed by it anyway. At least this way, we all have a fighting chance."

Laszlo and Isis shared a silent glance, each non-verbally asking the other's decision, but the stakes were high enough that they had both already decided.

"Alright, Admiral," Isis said, turning back to the screen. "So where's this bomb of yours?"

"I'll have it prepared for you by the time you reach the Orion's flight deck," Rigel replied. "I'd recommend you cloak now before you take off - no need to tip our hand anymore than we have to."

"I've ordered hangar control to begin transferring fuel back to the Wyvern," Captain Humboldt chimed in. "You have permission to launch as soon as you're ready. Good luck, you two."

"To all of us, Elgar."

*   *   *

The Orion had a lot of internal space, and Artemis remembered that it had been difficult to decide what to do with all of it. Even for as big as it was, there was only so much fuel it needed to carry, and only so many weapons they could reasonably arm it with. As such, almost a fifth of the dreadnought's interior had simply been designated as "cargo bays" for lack of any other suggestion. From time to time, some of this cargo took the form of various unusual or secretive things the Solar Navy had nowhere better to keep.

It was one of these things that Artemis was on her way to collect. The Interregnum had seen military technology pushed to its limits, as both sides sought to gain as much of an advantage over their enemy. The Orion was one of the products of this arms race, but only one of the most visible. The artificial intelligence known as the General had been unconcerned in its inscrutable calculations with many of the factors that held conventional nations back in munitions development, and it had devised its fair share of secret weapons as the war had turned against it. Artemis herself had dealt with quite a few of them over the course of the conflict, and the object she now stood before was the fruit of one such mission.

Anyone familiar with the antimatter industry would have recognised the device as a modified Penning-Malmberg tank: a device that used magnetic fields to safely confine the horrendously volatile substance in a vacuum. Aside from its antiquated design, it was basically the same as the tanks used by most starships in the known Galaxy to store antiproton fuel. What was strange about it were the numerous auxiliary safeguards that had been installed in the tank, far more stringent safety measures than such devices typically merited. The cargo bay itself was also sealed within a thick metal silo normally used for reactor construction, and the security systems keeping it locked would have put the most paranoid bank to shame.

Artemis didn't stop to study the PM tank or its surroundings, though. She had to work quickly, because one of the security measures was a keycard designed to melt itself down after a few minutes. As she slid it into its slot on the tank's control panel, its LCD display ticked away the seconds. She entered the randomised 20-digit access code, and waited as the terminal scanned her body. Satisfied that she matched its profile, the system beeped its assent and gave her a menu. Artemis selected her option and reached for one of the hefty canisters sitting in a rack off to one side, plugged into charging sockets. As she unplugged it, lights set into the heavy cylinder began glowing blue, changing to red as Artemis plugged it into a port in the PM tank's centre and pressed a button to begin filling it. Several seconds passed as material passed from tank to canister, until the machinery gave a buzz of completion. She yanked the canister free of the port, finding it to be twice as heavy when full, and pulled her access card out of the terminal. With less than a minute left on its clock, it was already beginning to turn grey and brittle, and as Artemis tossed it into a security incinerator by the silo door its shape was already crumbling into desiccated pieces.

With her package in hand, Artemis briskly made her way through the Orion to its hangar complex. The name hardly did it justice - it ran the full height of the ship and at least a third of its length, innumerable hangar bays and open flight decks surrounding a cavity big enough to comfortably accommodate any of the ships in the Solar Navy should they need repairs or refit. Technicians and engineers hurried to and fro across the flight decks, stricken warships hung in their berths awaiting emergency repairs, and squadrons of starfighters flocked around refuelling gantries. Anything smaller than a frigate was lost in the sheer scale of the complex, and the Wyvern was no exception. It sat in a remote corner of one of the decks, safely out of the way of the business of war.

Isis was standing at the base of the Wyvern's loading ramp, waiting for Artemis. For all her innate confidence, she was ill-at-ease about her surroundings - a career criminal like her preferred to stay as far away from official organisations like the Solar Navy as possible, and standing aboard its flagship was very much not doing that. The battle outside the ship, verging on apocalyptic as it was, wasn't helping matters in the slightest. The arrival of the hover-trolley carrying a tall robotic figure was a welcome distraction.

"Isis Lagato, I assume?" the figure greeted as she stepped off the trolley onto the deck. She carried the canister behind her and laid it at the foot of the loading ramp with a heavy clunk.

"That's me," Isis answered, "and you?"

"Call me Artemis. I have a present for you."

"Our super-bomb, I assume?"

Artemis nodded. "Indeed. This canister contains ten kilograms of an exotic substance called antithorium-232."

Isis furrowed her brow. "ANTIthorium? I've heard of thorium, but..."

"Yes, this is its antiparticle counterpart. It's a little something left over from the Interregnum - we're not sure exactly why or how the General went to the trouble of synthesising it, but based on its explosive yield we can probably hazard a guess as to its purpose."

Isis glanced nervously at the canister, with its many warning labels and pulsing status lights. "And, uh, what exactly is this thing's yield?"

"At a rough guess, I'd say up to ten gigatons."

Isis's eyes widened in shock. "HOW much?!"

"Ten gigatons. That's just an estimate, mind you - we've never actually conducted any physical weapons tests on it. In fact, this will be the first time we've ever detonated any of it - won't that be exciting?"

"That's not the word I'd use..." Isis muttered, resisting the urge to back away from the bomb. She cleared her throat and spoke up as she hefted the bomb up to bring it aboard. "So, are those battlegroups ready to go?"

"They are," Artemis confirmed as she took up the other end of the bomb. "As soon as you're on the move, they can clear you a path to the Wargod. We don't have any intel on its interior, so once you get inside you'll be on your own."

"I'm sure that'll be no problem. If this antithorium stuff is as nasty as you say it is, we probably just need to find the first thing that looks important and set it off, right?"

"As good as a plan as any. If nothing else, it should leave a sufficiently large hole to slow it down. Just remember to be careful with it."

"Don't worry, I usually am with horrifically explosive things."

"Glad to hear it. In any case, I think we'd both better get to it, then. Good luck out there."

"To both of us."

With that, Artemis left the Wyvern's cargo bay. Now alone, Isis set about securing the antithorium bomb. She did so gingerly, almost nervously, treating the device as though it were radioactive. Once satisfied that it wouldn't be going anywhere, she closed the loading ramp and made her way to the cockpit.

Laszlo was waiting at the copilot's station, and looked up as Isis entered. "I take it we've taken delivery of our super-bomb, then?"

"Mm-hmm. I've secured it in the cargo bay," Isis replied as she took the pilot's seat and ran through pre-launch checks. "Have you ever heard of something called "antithorium"?"

Laszlo looked thoughtful for a moment, then shrugged. "Doesn't ring a bell. Sounds like the antimatter version of thorium, though. That's what powering our bomb, is it?"

"That's what I've been told. Apparently, it has a ten gigaton yield."

Laszlo's eyes went as wide as saucers. "... and they're entrusting this thing to us?!"

"Looks like they've got a lot riding on us."

"Then let's not disappoint them, shall we?" Laszlo opened a comm channel. "Wyvern to Orion, do you read us?"

"Orion here, Wyvern, we read you," said the Lord Admiral's voice. "The battlegroups are in position to escort you to the target. Once you're on the move, let us know and they'll advance. Maintain radio silence from then on - the less chance the Wargod has of intercepting your transmissions, the better."

"Understood, Admiral. Good luck." Laszlo closed the channel, as the Wyvern lifted out of the hangar complex, vanishing in a haze of light, and into the battle raging all around. Commonwealth warships clustered around the Orion, ready to carve a path through the alien fleet to the colossus at its centre, still looming over the planetoid's surface.

As the battlegroups began to move out, Laszlo and Isis shared a glance. They flashed each other a confident grin.

"Let's roll."

Chapter 13

"Orion to battlegroups 1-Alpha-Six and 1-Beta-Nine, report status."

"This is SNV Trajan, all ships report combat readiness."

"SNV Mannerheim here, green status across the board."

"Acknowledged. Form up in spearhead formation, vectored at these coordinates."

Led by their dreadnought flagships, the battlegroups massed in their ready positions - heavy hitters clustered before the dreadnoughts at the centre, fast harriers and fighters in a shield wall around them, support ships and long-range guns bringing up the rear. All around the battlefield, other Commonwealth ships renewed their efforts, hoping to thin out the enemy line and give the spear a better chance of breaking through.

"Trajan to Orion, all ships in position. Ready to go at your command."

"Acknowledged, Trajan. Orion to all ships - spearhead, advance!"

The charge was slow at first, but as the massive capital ships got underway they picked up speed rapidly, dozens of powerful engines driving them forward. The frigates and fighters wove and dodged around the heavier capital ships, hoping to confound enemy targetting as they surged forward, drawing ever closer to the Sagittarian line. The Wargod's subordinate ships were already firing shots at the spearhead, trying to slow it down and cut it apart, but their numbers in the immediate vicinity were too thinned out to stop it completely.

The formations met, and tore into each other. The combat zone was a maelstrom of energy bolts and missiles as warships exchanged broadsides and strike craft chased each other down. Shields blazed and crackled, armour scorched and melted. Ships on both sides were destroyed and reduced to debris, but still the spearhead carried on forward.

"Trajan to all bombers - status report!"

"This is Italica Leader, bomber units at 97% strength."

"We've almost broken through the enemy line. Prime disruptor ordnance and prepare to launch."

"Roger, Trajan. All bomber units! Form up on me and prime EMPs."

The Commonwealth Estoc-class bomber was a hefty starfighter that could carry a lot of missiles and bombs, and dozens of them were converging from all corners of the fight, shadowed by their interceptor escorts. The flights of bombers drew into formation at the front of the spear, bearing down on the Wargod's underside. Most of the Wargod's ships had been committed to the conflict, leaving few to guard the colossus itself. They had a clear shot.

"EMPs, fire!"

Every bomber opened up, and from each of their ordnance bays their missiles poured out before them - dozens, scores, hundreds. They formed a thick swarm, twisting and dodging around each other as they rushed towards their target, as point-defense fire from the Wargod lashed out to swat them aside. The hail of turret fire thinned the swarm out a little, but there were far too many warheads to prevent them from finding their mark.

As the missiles slammed into the Wargod's shields, they each unleashed a storm of electrical energy. The effect of each impact merged with and fed off its neighbours, their combined power multiplying exponentially into a blue-white blaze of light. The Wargod's shield was glowing almost as brightly as lightning arced across its surface, until finally it was too much and the shield failed.

"Italica Leader to Trajan, EMP strike has opened up its shields!"

"Trajan to spearhead, attack pattern Troy!"

With the shields torn open, the ships of the spearhead flotilla massed around each other, finding the optimal attack vector, and opened fire. Through the shield gap they poured a maelstrom of gunfire and ordnance. Even on the incredibly thick armour of the Wargod it took its toll. But there was something unusual about the pattern of weapons fire - there was a distinct gap in the firing pattern, big enough for a small ship to fly through, almost as if the Commonwealth ships were being careful not to hit something.

"Vice Admiral, I'm picking up readings from the Wargod's shield systems. I think it's recharging!"

"Admiral, sensors are detecting several enemy ships on an intercept course. We're going to be surrounded in a minute."

"Trajan to spearhead, break off attack and withdraw back to the fleet! We've done everything we can."

As the ships of the spearhead turned away from the Wargod and headed back through the Sagittarian line, Vice Admiral Elrey spared a glance through the windows of the Trajan's bridge at the Wargod. It's up to them now, he thought, and I hope they're up to it...

*   *   *

"That may be the most I've ever been shot at," Laszlo remarked, as the spearhead's assault dwindled behind the Wyvern. "Remind me again why I agreed to all this?"

"Shot AROUND," corrected Isis, not looking away from her controls, "it's an important distinction."

"That doesn't make me any happier to see that much gunfire on sensors. Speaking of sensors... I think I see an entry point in the top of the hangar, past that cruiser."

"I see it. Bringing us in."

The Wyvern flew up into the Wargod's shipyard complex, dodging around Sagittarian ships and the debris left by the spearhead's assault, safely ignored by the enemy flotilla. Up close, there was an almost organic look to the Wargod's architecture - the design and arrangement of its components melded together as if all its metal and polymer had grown into place, instead of simply being assembled. Exposed structural girders protruded like bone from panelling seemingly stretched between them like skin, covering up cables and ducts that resembled blood vessels and muscle fibres.

The Wyvern flew on through a rent in the hangar's ceiling torn open by the attack. As they passed the outer layers of armour and hull plating, Laszlo and Isis found themselves surrounded by a honeycomb lattice of support struts wrapped around massive tubes that stretched out into the deep shadows of the Wargod's lightless interior.

Laszlo gazed out at the spectacle, and couldn't help but be unnerved. If the sheer size of the Wargod hadn't already made him feel small, then its innards' uncanny resemblance to flesh and bone certainly did. He swallowed nervously and looked over at Isis. "Is this how a bacterium feels inside someone's body, d'you suppose?"

Isis glanced briefly back at him, diverting her gaze from the controls for only a moment. "That might not be a bad idea, actually. These tubes could run all across the ship."

"How can you be sure?"

"I can't, but this thing's got to have some way of moving power and resources around... maintenance ducts, or something like that. You'd need a decent infrastructure to operate a ship this big."

"So... break into one and follow it 'til we find something important?"

"It's the best chance we've got. Find me an opening."

Laszlo turned back to his sensors and began searching. "Hmmmm... I see what looks like an access hatch, but no external controls. Time for Plan B."

"Plan B... ?"

Laszlo flashed a grin. "B for "blow it open"!"

Isis rolled her eyes and shrugged. "So much for stealth."

If the Wyvern had been visible, it might have been possible to see a secret panel in one of the wings retracting to reveal a hidden compartment filled with missiles. As one of those missiles launched, it was definitely visible, even more so as it detonated and destroyed the access hatch. While the white light of the explosion faded, the Wyvern wasted no time and dove right in.

A squadron of small drones came flying down the tube towards them. They narrowly missed hitting the Wyvern as it deftly manoeuvred through their formation, but they were only the first. As the Wyvern flew full-bore down the tube, steady streams of drones made their way in the other direction, weaving up-and-down and side-to-side.

"Looks like maintenance drones," Isis guessed, not looking away from piloting. "Antibodies, to go with your bacterium metaphor."

"They must be looking for us - trying to flush us out," Laszlo observed.

"If we do find something to hit, they're going to make it difficult to set the bomb."

"It'll be a lot easier if they have something else to chase down. What say I hop in the Eaglehawk and draw them off?"

"Are you sure you can handle them?"

"I was top of my class at the Academy for fighter training, remember? I can take 'em!"

"If you say so. Get on it, Las."

Laszlo leapt out of his seat, cloak swishing behind him, and hurried through the ship to the hangar bay, where the Eaglehawk sat waiting. It was a Claymore-class heavy starfighter that Laszlo had begun his pirate career by stealing. Practically the crown jewel of the Naval Fighter Corps, it was large, fast, and heavily armed, and it was exactly the kind of firepower that Laszlo needed to deal with the drones. He pulled its key from his belt as he dashed around the fighter's wing tip and thumbed the unlock button. The cockpit canopy slid open, and he vaulted deftly over the side and squarely into the pilot's seat. By swift and almost reflexive motion he inserted the key, entered his passcode, and activated the ignition sequence. The Eaglehawk's dual reactors came to life as Laszlo fastened his seatbelt, sealed the canopy, and seized the flight controls. As the hangar door opened before it, the Eaglehawk lifted itself off the deck on its manoeuvring thrusters and retracted its landing gear. Laszlo's eyes were fixed on the launch diagnostic readout. The moment the last system entry turned green, he opened up the throttle.

The drones reacted the very instant the Eaglehawk exited the Wyvern's cloaking field. As the fighter rocketed through the tube, the drones peeled away from their flight paths en masse and surged after it. Tiny and light, they were able to keep pace with the Eaglehawk and its powerful engines, forming up in a roiling swarm behind it. As they encroached upon the Eaglehawk, they activated their cutting tools and began attacking the fighter's shields. Alone, the cutting beams wouldn't do much to the Eaglehawk, but there were dozens of them, and more were slowly gaining.

Laszlo glanced at the shield display in his HUD as the rear shield began flashing, and flicked at the gunnery controls in his joystick. He selected a weapon and a semitransparent rear-view image appeared on the HUD, showing Laszlo the swarm of drones behind him. Targetting reticles swept across the image, but the horde was so thick that he hardly needed to aim. He pulled the trigger and fired the Eaglehawk's rear-facing cannons. A storm of plasma bolts slammed into the drones and carved through their formation. Most of the ones up front were destroyed outright, and the drones behind them were forced to slow down as their flight path was choked with debris. While they picked their way through the remains, the Eaglehawk accelerated away down the tube, just slowly enough to let the faster drones keep on its tail.

Back in the Wyvern's cockpit, Isis watched as the knot of drones took off after the Eaglehawk, and away from the Wyvern. With her flightpath clear, she took the ship deeper into the Wargod's interior. As its sensors scanned its surroundings and built up a picture of the dreadnought's structure, it became clear that the massive tube was part of an intricate network that ran throughout the ship. More shafts merged together and branched off from each other, winding around and leading into sections of densely packed machinery. But Isis still couldn't discern any familiar logic to the ship's design - she hadn't seen any signs of life or habitation, no indication that any of this had been built with a crew in mind. If nothing else, it made finding a viable target tricky. With no obvious purpose to anything, Isis was forced to rely on energy readings to guide her, following the power conduits that criss-crossed throughout the system of tubes.

It was a long time before Isis found something in the maze of branching tubes, but it was clear that the power conduits were converging in one location, leading her into a vast spherical chamber. As the Wyvern flew in, a tremendous machine came into view - through the sphere's vertical axis ran a massive column covered in intricate and inscrutable mechanical detail, in the middle of which was a transparent bubble. It was difficult to see what was inside the bubble past the electrical energy constantly crackling within it, but it seemed to be emanating from a glowing point suspended in a cage-like structure. What readings the Wyvern could detect from all this made virtually no sense to Isis - she couldn't even guess at the scientific principles at play here - but the incredible energy signature this thing was giving off left her in no doubt that it was a power generator. This is our weak point, thought Isis.

The Wargod had no intention of making this easy, however. Flying throughout the chamber were dozens, maybe even hundreds of drones, swirling around the generator like a tornado. Squadrons of drones deftly wove in and out of each other's flightpaths, filling the space surrounding the generator with their metal bodies. There was no way the Wyvern would be able to squeeze through without being detected, if not outright torn to pieces.

Isis called up a comm channel. "Las, are you still alive?"

"Still kicking, Isis. What's the situation?"

"I've found a large generator, but it's surrounded by drones - more than I think I can fight. I need another distraction."

"I don't suppose you can send me a map or something? This place is a bloody labyrinth."

"Sure. Transmitting it now."

There was a long pause as the data transferred from the Wyvern to the Eaglehawk, and Laszlo pored over it. "... alright, I think I can get to you. See you in a bit!"

Laszlo closed the channel and studied the maps from both the Wyvern and the Eaglehawk's sensors. A quick route to Isis's weak point wasn't too difficult to figure out, but it meant turning around and retracing some of his steps, and there were still dozens of drones on his tail, with more joining all the time even as he took out a few with his rear cannons. Luckily, these were far from the fighter's only weapons.

Laszlo flipped the Eaglehawk over to face the swarm and selected the anti-fighter missiles. He fired several into the horde of drones, destroying many and scattering the rest, before gunning the engines and ploughing straight through them. Debris bounced off the Eaglehawk's forward shields, and the surviving drones quickly reoriented themselves and took off after it again.

It was several minutes before the Eaglehawk rejoined the Wyvern, tearing through the bulkheads to reach the generator chamber. The heavy fighter's explosive entrance had precisely the desired effect - the swarms of drones immediately pulled away from protecting the generator and chased after the intruder. Laszlo responded with cannon fire and missiles a-plenty, and began taking them on a merry chase throughout the generator complex.

"Bloody hell, there's a lot of those things..." he muttered to himself as he rebalanced his shields. "You should be clear now, Isis, but make it quick! I can't hold all these things off forever!"

Isis didn't need to be told twice. As soon as the drones had left their protective flight, she had set the Wyvern to take itself in close to the generator's surface. Even as it did so, she dashed back to her quarters and got geared up in her stealthsuit in record time. Now dressed for the occasion, she hurried to the cargo bay and over to the door controls. Everything dwindled into silence as she evacuated the air in the bay, save for the sound of her own breathing. As the floor hatch opened to reveal the generator chamber, Isis was struck by its sheer size - without the windows of the ship insulating her from it, she had a sudden visceral sense of its sheer magnitude, and her insignificance in comparison. She didn't have time to feel intimidated though, pushing the feeling to the back of her mind as she strode over to where she had secured the antithorium bomb. Unlike her and the Wyvern it didn't have a cloaking device, so she could only hope that the drones were too busy trying to deal with Laszlo to see it. She could at least switch off its ever-pulsing warning lights, which she did as she hefted the thing over to the open hatch. She looked down at the machinery of the generator for a moment, before letting herself fall forward out of the ship.

Free from the Wyvern's internal gravity, she and the bomb tumbled out into the chamber together, before she grabbed a control from her belt. As she switched it on, microthrusters built into her suit flashed into life and arrested her movement. She twiddled the control's thumbstick for a moment and adjusted her grip on the bomb, trying to find a comfortable way of guiding it down. After a moment, she settled on straddling the thing as though she were riding it, and flared her thrusters to send her and her mount towards the generator.

The machinery was no less inscrutable up close, as the smaller details resolved into focus the closer Isis came to the generator, heading toward where the column met the sphere. A few metres from it, she released her hold on the bomb, slowing up just a little as it carried on. It gently hit the surface and bounced back, until Isis pushed it down and engaged its grav-clamps. She floated over the bomb and began setting its timer. She paused for just a moment over the controls, taking a deep breath, and set the bomb to count down. She shoved off and looked back up where she'd come from. The form of the cloaked Wyvern was superimposed in wireframe on her suit's HUD, allowing her to thrust back up towards it, rather faster than before now that the bomb wasn't weighing her down.

As Isis shot back up into the Wyvern's cargo bay, she grabbed the hatch's edge and clambered back into the ship's gravity field. She didn't stop to wait as the room sealed and repressurised, instead carrying on to the cockpit. She pulled off her helmet and settled back into the pilot's seat, before pulling the Wyvern away and opening a comm channel.

"Bomb is set, Las. Time for us to go."

"And not a moment too soon," came Laszlo's reply, "I think I've had about all the fun these things have to offer."

Laszlo pointed the Eaglehawk at the entry wound he had come in through and let loose a tremendous hail of missiles in all directions, throwing the swarms of drones into disarray and giving him a chance to slip away. By the time the drones were able to start following, the Eaglehawk was already back in the system of tubes and heading away fast. Lining up and matching speeds with a target only the Eaglehawk could see, Laszlo pushed forward into the Wyvern's waiting hangar. Its interior appeared around the canopy as though a veil had been lifted as it passed into the cloaking field. Once his fighter was landed, Laszlo wasted no time jumping out and ran back to the Wyvern's cockpit.

"How are we doing, Isis?" he asked upon entering, dropping down into the copilot's seat.

"Just fine, Las. We're well on course to get out of here. How's the Eaglehawk?"

"A little scratched up, but nothing serious. Those drones aren't fighters, but there were a lot of them. How long do we have?"

"I set the bomb's timer for ten minutes..."

"Oh good, plenty of time."

"... but I also set up a proximity trigger, in case they try to defuse it."

"Oh... then let's hope we fly faster than they notice things."

*   *   *

Though many of the maintenance drones had been taken out by Laszlo's attack, most of them had survived intact. A lot of them had followed his escape to track his ship down, but the ship had disappeared as suddenly as it had appeared. As some of the drones trawled through the tubes to try to uncover the intruders, others remained behind to repair damage inflicted to the generator complex, restoring shot-out plating and clearing away the debris of their destroyed brethren. The generator itself had escaped the fighter's stray gunfire, with barely a shot landed on it. Only a handful of drones were spared to see to it, roving up and down its structure and examining its systems for repairs that were needed.

One of the drones circled around the spherical body of the generator's core, only to detect a foreign object attached nearby. It approached and focused its sensors on it - it was a cylindrical object that was generating an energy signature. It wasn't clear what it was, but it definitely didn't belong here. The drone extended its manipulator claws and reached out to grab it...

*   *   *

Explosions in space are not like those that happen on a planet's surface. Without air or gravity there are no billowing plumes of flame or columns of smoke - instead there is simply a sphere of energy, blinding light spreading out in all directions, forcing aside whatever debris isn't outright vaporised. It was this that the bridge crew of the Orion witnessed the Wargod undergo - a massive explosion overtook the main body of the colossal ship, tearing unimpeded through armour and weapon emplacements like a tsunami. Smaller detonations flared up ahead of the main blast as volatile systems and ordnance overloaded. Pieces big and small were split off and hurled away from the main body of the vessel, trailing fragments of hull behind them as they disintegrated.

A cheer went up among the Orion's officers as the Wargod crumbled, but the Admiral didn't join in. A grim feeling was coiling in the back of his mind as he looked out at the sundered hulk listing in the midst of its own debris. In spite of the magnitude of the antithorium's detonation, too much of it had remained intact for his liking.

He turned to one of his bridge crew. "Ms. Vercet, I want a status report on that thing."

Vercet studied her console for a moment. "I'm still getting power readings from the main mass of the wreckage, but its shields are down and its weapons don't seem to be responding. The alien fleet is still fighting-- no, scratch that, they're going into retreat. They're heading back to the Wargod."

The Admiral called up the sensors on his own console. Indeed, the various ships of the Wargod's fleet were withdrawing in waves from the fight and converging on their mothership at full speed. He assumed they were simply forming a defensive perimeter, but the ships were lining up far too close for that to be the case, almost as if they were landing on it. Rigel sent the image to the bridge's main holoprojector and zoomed in. A wing of alien cruisers were clustering around some of the inscrutable machinery in the Wargod's now-revealed interior. The ships flew as close as they could to the structure, almost rubbing up against it, until suddenly they began to lose their shape. They disintegrated into fragments as though they were melting, and those fragments were drawn into the guts of the machinery. Holes were patched up, missing pieces grew back, and lights flickered back into life as the machine put itself back together.

"Oh god... they're repairing that thing!"

The Admiral zoomed the image back out, and it became quickly apparent that many more ships were also surrendering their forms to restore their command ship. Already the machinery the ships were merging into looked as good as new.

"Admiral, something's happening to KV-649-B's surface - it's being drawn up into the Wargod's remains!"

True to Vercet's report, fragments of the planet were breaking off and flying up towards the Wargod. A cone of rock and dust was drawing itself into a massive aperture in the rear of the dreadnought. As material flowed into it, the regrowth of the ship's structure began in earnest, far faster than the piecemeal disassembly of its fleet would allow. Even from the safe distance that the Orion had from it, the Wargod's reconstruction was gradual but clearly visible.

"Admiral, projections indicate that it won't be long before the Wargod restores its combat capability. Do we press the attack?"

The Admiral continued silently gazing at the regrowing colossus for a moment, his emotions all but unreadable. "No. Have all ships continue maintaining a safe distance." He tore his gaze away and bent over his console. "I'm putting a stop to this right now," he snarled to himself. He pulled a key out and inserted it into a hidden slot on the console. The control panel slid aside in sections to reveal another beneath, this one centred around a single large button. On the screen above it a new window opened, asking for a passcode. He entered a long string of digits, and after a moment of processing it was accepted. The window widened and displayed a heading: "BLACK SHIELD: OFFLINE". Figures, statistics, and other data were arrayed beneath, with a small subwindow that read "Device status: ready. Activate?". The Admiral selected "yes".

The Orion's front section was encased in a thick layer of armour, giving its prow something of a beak-like appearance. Part of that prow was now opening up, hefty panels moving aside to uncover a strange device. Mounted between a pair of spindly pylons was a set of three concentric metal rings, the largest of which was easily four kilometres across. Between the bases of the pylons an array of strangely designed emitters pointed out at the rings, aimed at their centre. The lights of the emitters pulsed as they activated, and the rings turned in their gantry to delineate the axes of a sphere.

On the Admiral's screen, diagnostic readouts scrolled rapidly by as everything came online. He leant on the console impatiently as he watched the information flash past. Eventually the window's heading changed: "BLACK SHIELD: READY". The Admiral stood up and began typing quickly. He finished up by jabbing the panel's central button, and the screen responded by telling him "Charging sequence in progress..."

The Admiral opened a channel to the entire fleet. "Orion to all ships, we are preparing to fire an exotic weapon. Clear the Orion's forward firing arc at once! There will be a severe gravitic hazard in the area. Repeat, we are firing an exotic weapon - clear the Orion's forward firing arc at once." He closed the channel and turned to his bridge crew. "Helm, orient the Orion to face the Wargod head-on. Put it in the dead centre of our firing arc."

As the dreadnought turned, the rings of the Black Shield device began to spin. They quickly picked up speed, and as they turned into a spherical blur of metal the emitters pointing at their centre began to glow brightly. At their focal point between the whirling rings, space began to contract on itself, warping torturously in a way usually only attainable by the death throes of the largest stars.

As this was happening, the Navy fleet had wasted no time in clearing the way for the Orion's shot. The Sagittarian fleet saw their opportunity and began to bear down on the Orion, regarding the flagship as too important a target to ignore. If their sensors saw what the Black Shield was producing then it didn't stop them descending upon the Orion's location in droves.

The Admiral watched the Sagittarian advance on the bridge's tactical map, occasionally glancing at the mind-boggling figures the Black Shield's readout rattled off at him. He didn't pay much attention to it - now wasn't the time for him to be trying to comprehend astrophysics on this order - until a new window popped up, flashing an urgent red, bearing the text "BLACK SHIELD FULLY CHARGED. SINGULARITY DESTABILISATION IMMINENT!".

The Admiral stretched his hand out over the control panel's central button. He gave the Sagittarians on the tactical map one last look, flexed his fingers, and pressed the button.

The rings of the Black Shield device slowed to a stop and faced outward, extending into a makeshift barrel. The singularity hung in place, invisible save for the severe lensing its gravity produced, until a pulse of force flashed through the rings and ejected it at tremendous speed.

As the projectile approached them, the ships at the head of the Sagittarian formation flew aside to avoid it. The smallest and fastest ships dodged it easily, but the slower vessels behind them were not so lucky. They were dragged out of their flightpath by the singularity, bits and pieces of their hull torn off and drawn into its inescapable grasp. As more mass was trapped in its gravity well, the singularity was wreathed in an ever-building plume of debris, heated into incandescence by unimaginable tidal forces. The Sagittarian formation quickly realised what was coming their way and went into panic mode, diverting their flight outward and away from the singularity. The Wargod itself could not escape, however, too large and too incomplete to move away.

Fragments of hull and chunks of substructure peeled away from the Wargod's prow as the singularity bore down on the colossus. It plowed straight into it as though its armour wasn't even there, and it very quickly wasn't as the singularity's pull tore it inward. The structure of the Wargod warped and crumbled away as the singularity passed through the vessel and consumed it, the red-hot blaze of its accretion disk casting a hellish light on its pieces in the brief moments before they were annihilated.

Even the sheer size of the Wargod could only last so long as its mass was absorbed by the singularity, increasing its gravitation and drawing in even more matter in a vicious cycle. Within minutes, it was all over. The ancient alien dreadnought was gone, and its remains within the accretion disk dwindled gradually away. The singularity lingered for a little while, but this high in KV-649-2's orbit there was no more mass to absorb. Too small to sustain itself, the singularity eventually shrank away to nothing, and its last wisps of Hawking radiation were the final epitaph of the Wargod.

Chapter 14

After the Wargod had emerged from the anomaly, Morgan Strannik and his pirate cohort had scrambled back into their shuttle and fled into lightspeed as soon as the ship had reached orbit. As wise a decision as it may have been, what Professor Kellermann certainly didn't appreciate about it was that they had left him behind. Alone in the Sagittarian facility, he couldn't help but feel rather slighted that he should figure so small in their thoughts. Still, aside from activating his spacesuit's emergency beacon and hoping for rescue, there was nothing to be done about it. To pass the time, he started to explore the facility, taking notes on what he found to plan for future expeditions, though he stayed away from pressing any more buttons.

Kellermann didn't know how long he'd spent exploring, but as he stepped back into the hangar he saw a ship on the horizon. For a moment he feared that Strannik had come back to collect him, but as the ship came closer it became obvious that it wasn't his shuttle. It was much too clean, for one thing.

The ship drew ponderously up to the hangar bay, hanging in the thin air as if examining it. Kellermann recognised some of its markings as Solar Navy, but its guns were also a bit of a giveaway. Kellermann waved to the pilot and stepped back against one wall. The pilot didn't wave back, but they took the gunship into the hangar and set it down. After a few moments, the nearest hatch opened up to admit a pair of marines. Stepping out into the hangar, their eyes swept the area, but with no pirates in the area they held their rifles at ease. Satisfied that there were no enemies around, one of them stepped up to Kellermann.

"Professor Lorentz Kellermann?"

"That's me," Kellermann answered, "and may I say, I've never been so glad to see a soldier."

"Glad to hear it, sir. Are you injured?"

"No, I'm fine, just quite shaken. Do you have some way of contacting the CAI? I'd best update them."

"You can use the comm onboard the gunship, sir. If you're ready to leave, we'll return to the Orion at once."

Kellermann nodded and gratefully followed the marines onto the gunship. One of them pointed him in the direction of the ship's comm station, and he fell into the seat heavily, the weight of the past few hours really starting to hit him. As the gunship's hatch closed and the craft lifted off, Kellermann unsealed his helmet and dropped it to one side, before dialling the frequency of Eurus Station.

The face of the station commander appeared on the screen after only a moment's wait, and broke into a relieved smile. "Professor Kellermann! It's wonderful to see you alive!"

"It's pretty wonderful to be alive, too, thank you," Kellermann replied. "It seems the situation here has calmed down. The Solar Navy has rescued me - I daresay I'll be back shortly."

"We'll be glad to have you back. What happened to you out there?"

Kellermann sighed and ran a hand through his thinning hair. "Well... to make a long story short, I watched the opening of the Wargod's Tomb."

"Th-- the Tomb?!" The station commander stared agog. "You mean it's real?!"

"I was as surprised as you. I'm sure the Navy will want to scour the site first, but I suppose we'll have to organise a research expedition."

"Of course! This could be the discovery of the century! I can't overstate how exciting this is!"

"Oh yes, tremendously exciting. Though to be honest, all I feel right now is tired."

"I can well imagine, Professor. We'll be sure to notify all personnel not to disturb you once you return."

"Yes, thank you. I've been disturbed quite enough to be getting on with. I'm just glad the pirates are gone..."

*   *   *

"So... how bad is the damage?" Morgan Strannik's voice was very level, considering how badly things were going for him.

"Zsech says the entire power network is shot to hell," Ankerak grimly reported, xir antennae curling. "The primary generator is basically in pieces - if we try to use it, she'll says it'll probably blow up - the FTL capacitors have been overloaded, and half the engines are burnt out. We're dead in the water."

"Right." Morgan gave a long sigh and slumped back in his command chair. The power loop restart trick he'd pulled off on the Commonwealth cruiser was a gamble, and it seemed the Corsair's luck had run out. "Did she give any kind of estimate about restoring any kind of functionality?"

"She said she'll work on it, but... well, I won't repeat exactly what she said, but without spare parts she says she doesn't think there's much chance of getting anything running."

Morgan's face was contorted with frustration but he managed to swallow it back down, knowing full well that it wouldn't help with the matter at hand. "Fine. Do we have communications? Emergency beacons?"

"Yes, we have both. But we're pretty far off the beaten path. We're not getting a strong enough signal from the Undernet to hook into, and if we try public networks, the Navy will probably find us."

"It's our best chance right now, if Zsech can't do her job."

"Aye, Cap'n. Er... there is one more thing."

"Of course there is. Let's hear it."

"Some of the crew are... less than happy about our situation. They're questioning your leadership."

"Well, isn't that interesting..."

Morgan got to his feet and unholstered his pistol.

"You work on getting communications working. Looks like I'll be busy laying down the law."

"Aye-aye, sir. Call me down if you need any support."

"I'll be fine. You just hold down the fort in case the Solar Navy tracks us down or something."

*   *   *

"Considering everything that went down here, it would be difficult to track down anything, Captain."

"I understand that, Lord Admiral, but... well, the Orion's sensors are probably the most powerful in the Navy, I was hoping..."

"... that we could ascertain the status of the Wyvern?"

Elgar nodded to the Admiral, his hands fidgeting sheepishly. Both officers were sitting in their respective offices, seeing to the administration that followed any engagement.

"I know this isn't a high priority at present, but Laszlo... well, he stills means a lot to me, I can't deny it. It would be good to know, one way or the other."

"I understand, Captain. Unfortunately, the Orion isn't really in a position to see any more than the Durendal. I'm not at liberty to discuss the nature of the weapons involved, but they didn't really leave anything to study. No debris, no ion trails... even FTL traces were wiped clean."

"I see." Elgar was quiet, not meeting the Admiral's gaze.

"I'm sorry I don't have better news to give, Captain. If nothing else though, their actions may well have helped save billions, maybe trillions of lives."

"I suppose that's true," Elgar observed, feeling a little heartened by the thought. "In spite of everything, they're heroes."

"They certainly are, Captain. And so are you and everyone on your crew."

"Oh, well, thank you Admiral, but it's just part of the job, really."

The Admiral gave a little chuckle. "Technically yes, but I think staring down giant space monsters is a little outside your usual job description. There's no need for modesty today - you deserve to feel proud of what you've helped accomplish."

Elgar sat up a little straighter. "Thank you, sir."

"You're welcome, Captain. I should get back to it for now, though. If I do find any trace of the Wyvern, I'll be sure to pass it along. Orion out."

The two exchanged salutes, and the Admiral closed the connection. Captain Humboldt drummed his fingers on his desk for a moment as he processed his feelings. It seemed strange, given how long he'd resented Laszlo, to feel so invested in his well-being now. It had been quite an interesting time, he concluded as he rose to his feet and left his office.

The rest of the Durendal's bridge officers were already in position, though there was little for them to do while the ship was still in dock. Once the Wargod had been taken out, the rest of the Sagittarian fleet had fallen into disarray. Without their flagship commanding them, cleaning them up was a trivial task. All that remained was to repair the Navy fleet, and to that end they were arrayed above the Orion's hangar complex, patiently queueing up for the next available berth.

Captain Humboldt settled into his chair. "How are the repairs coming, Mx. Leurak?"

"The Orion estimates another five minutes before we're at 100%, sir," Leurak answered. "Vice Admiral Elrey has requested that we report back to the battlegroup as soon as we're able."

"Very well." Humboldt turned to the navigator. "Mr. Sandersby, I assume you've already prepared a course?"

"I certainly have, Captain," Sandersby replied. "Once we're clear of the Orion, we can prepare for the jump at your command."

"Excellent. Stand by for now."

A silence filled the bridge after that. Elgar stared idly out of the windows, as one cruiser lifted out of its berth to make way for another, his thoughts still chasing around in his mind.

"Captain?"

"Hmm?" Leurak's voice snapped Elgar out of his distraction. "What is it, Commander?"

"You seem troubled by something, Captain. Everything alright?"

"Yes, everything's fine. Just... thinking over the last few days, you know."

"This is about Hadron, isn't it?"

Elgar stared at Leurak for a moment. "Emara talked, didn't she?"

"She, er, might have done."

"Well, you're not wrong. Even after everything that split us apart, he was my friend once. The possibility of him dying like this..."

"Well, look at it this way, sir: he's wriggled out of capture repeatedly over the years - he and Lagato always have a way out. It's quite likely that they've got out this time too."

Elgar mulled this over, then gave a little laugh. "You know, I've never been so happy about that." His smile turned into a frown. "Although, if he doesn't resurface and surrender the Wyvern again, I guess that's his provisional pardon off the table."

Leurak shrugged, which was quite something to see on a species with four arms. "He surprised us once by cooperating with this whole business. Maybe he'll surprise us again in future."

"I suppose that's all I can hope for. Thank you for your insight, Commander."

"Any time, Captain."

"I suppose it's only a matter of time before we find out. I'm sure someone's looking for them..."

*   *   *

"Unfortunately, we've lost track of Hadron and Lagato. It's unclear what exactly became of them - the nature of the Black Shield device means that any trace of their ship would have been absorbed by the singularity, be it an FTL trace or debris."

Agent CE362 sat in the meeting room of their ship, addressing the voices of their superiors. With the matter of the Wargod resolved, they had taken their leave of the Durendal, heading off to whatever secretive business the Department had next on their docket.

"The use of the Black Shield will cause quite a stir in the galactic community, I think," one of the faceless voices remarked. "Not to mention the antithorium. How will the Lord Admiral deal with the political consequences of his decisions?"

"I don't expect those consequences will go very far," another voice answered. "The treaties regarding both superweapons and the Orion itself do have clauses regarding extreme circumstances - and the Wargod was quite an extreme circumstance, I'm sure you'll all agree."

"As for the Wargod, did anything survive the Black Shield?"

"Very little. However, what we have collected could be very intriguing," CE362 reported. "It's en-route to a secure facility as we speak."

"Excellent. The analysis will be interesting, I'm sure. And the Sagittarian facility?"

"Empty for now, though I'm sure Professor Kellermann will be arranging archaeological expeditions soon."

"Then the pirates are the only remaining loose ends?"

"Yes. Morgan Strannik is not likely to remain at liberty for long - the Corsair was damaged in its capture, and its escape would have strained its systems badly."

"But no actionable leads on the Wyvern?"

"None, sir. We have agents searching, and we believe the Lord Admiral does too. But it will be a difficult search for either party..."

*   *   *

Artemis wasn't in the habit of gambling, but in tracking down the Wyvern it was her only option. The Lord Admiral had given her a copy of the Orion's battle telemetry, but there was only a brief glimpse of what could have been the Wyvern before the antithorium explosion had blotted out the readings - and the Black Shield had wiped anything else away soon after. From that smidgen of data she had done her best to extrapolate the Wyvern's possible vector for an FTL jump, but a lot of it was simple guesswork. She suspected that as soon as they had found themselves in safe space, Hadron and Lagato would make another FTL jump to keep any pursuers off their trail, and with the leisure of not having an exploding dreadnought behind them would take steps to cover their tracks. If she didn't find them now, then one way or another they were gone.

Sitting at the controls of her own ship, Artemis stared steadily out at metaspace as the vessel passed through it. If she was superstitious she might have crossed her fingers, but it would have made operating the controls a bit tricky. Eventually her ship dropped back into normal space, and she immediately set the sensors to sweep the area. She hadn't been expecting to see the Wyvern waiting for her right there, and indeed the ship was nowhere to be seen for several light-years. There was something promising, though: an FTL jump trace, heavily degraded and badly distorted, but enough for her ship to extrapolate. As the figures were calculated, Artemis immediately began charging the capacitors for another jump, and set off as soon as she could after them.

The jump led her to empty space between stars. In an area like this there was probably nothing bigger than a stray hydrogen atom for several light-years. Artemis turned back to the sensors to check... there! A starship, bright and clear on the EMDAR. No-one would have a reason to be out here, so it could only be the Wyvern.

She opened a channel and sent out a message. "This is Artemis to the Wyvern. I'm here under my own initiative, not at Naval behest. Please respond."

There was no response for several seconds. The Wyvern was still, its shields at full but its cloak not active. Eventually, the message was accepted.

"I think I recognise your voice. You helped us out on Earth, didn't you?"

"And you gave us that antithorium bomb as well."

"Yes, that was me on both occasions. We didn't have time to get properly acquainted, alas."

On Artemis's screen, a splitscreen image of both Laszlo and Isis appeared. Isis nodded to herself in recognition.

"Yep, that's her. I think we're safe."

"And you're definitely not with the Navy?" Laszlo asked.

"Not since the Interregnum - I retired after the Commonwealth made... certain decisions. I'm sure you know the ones I mean, Laszlo."

Laszlo cocked an eyebrow knowingly. "Is that so?"

"But having said that, I still have friends in the Navy, and I lend a hand from time to time when the need arises."

"Are you saying things like the Wargod happen a lot?" Isis asked with more than a hint of incredulity.

"No, actually this was a pretty unusual one. I can't say that's a bad thing, though."

"You and me both, Artemis," Laszlo agreed. "I can't even imagine what would have happened if we hadn't sorted it out."

"I can," Artemis said grimly, "and it wouldn't have been pretty. It wouldn't just have been the Solar Commonwealth on the chopping block - the Suura Republic, the Tygoethan Clans, the Syohar Union... realistically, none of them would have stood a chance either. This entire quadrant of the Galaxy might have been scoured clean of civilisation. The final death toll could easily have numbered well into the trillions."

"Jesus Christ..." Isis muttered, "are you serious?"

"Oh yes. Remember that as far as the CAI can tell, the Sagittarian Empire was at least as powerful, if not more so, than the Solar Empire at its height. And look what the Wargod left of them."

"Why would they even build something like that? What could possibly justify it?"

"My guess would be an unprecedented existential threat, something that would itself be capable of destroying the Empire. It's hard to imagine anything else meriting such an investment of resources."

"Whatever reason they made for building that thing, I'm just glad it's gone," Laszlo said.

"As am I, Laszlo, and it can't go unremarked that you two were instrumental in ending that threat. That's why I tracked you down - on behalf of myself and certain friends of mine, I wanted to thank you for everything you've done."

Laszlo smirked. "That seems like a lot of effort to go to just for the sake of a thank-you note."

"Maybe so, but your efforts deserve recognition nonetheless. People on the right side of the law like Captain Humboldt will get ceremonies and medals and the like, but that's not possible for people of your... profession. But it's no exaggeration to say that you both may well have helped the Galaxy. Every citizen in the Commonwealth owes you a tremendous debt. So, thank you."

"Well, you're welcome, Artemis," Isis answered with a jocular salute. "And hey, if you ever need the Galaxy saved from any more big space monsters, let us know!"

"I'll definitely bear your names in mind."

"Er, one more thing," interrupted Laszlo. "Technically, we're not supposed to be out here with the Wyvern and all that... you're not going to snitch on our escape, are you?"

"Snitch on what, Laszlo? I have no idea what you're talking about." One of Artemis's eyelights shut off briefly in an electronic wink, before she started operating her ship's controls. "Well, I've said my piece. I'm sure you have business to attend to elsewhere, so I'll take my leave of you. Maybe we'll see each other again. Farewell."

With one last wave, the channel closed, and Artemis's ship jumped into FTL. Once more, the Wyvern was alone.

"Well, that was nice, wasn't it?" Laszlo remarked.

"Very nice, I thought," Isis agreed. "So, do we have any business to attend to elsewhere?"

"Not that I can recall just at the moment. Even if we did, it can wait - I think we could both do with a break."

"Best idea I've heard all day." Isis took hold of the Wyvern's controls. "So, where to?"

Laszlo shrugged. "No idea. Somewhere with a warm beach and cool drinks, for preference."

With that vague guidance, the Wyvern turned to face a distant destination, and headed off into the stars...

Printed in Great Britain
by Amazon